Loving Donovan

Also by Bernice L. McFadden

Sugar
The Warmest December
This Bitter Earth

Bernice L. McFadden

Loving Donovan

A Novel in Three Stories

Dutton

DUTTON
Published by the Penguin Group
Penguin Putnam Inc., 375 Hudson Street, New York, New York 10014, U.S.A.
Punguin Books Ltd, 80 Strand, London WC2R 0RL, England
Penguin Books Australia Ltd, 250 Camberwell Road, Camberwell, Victoria 3124, Australia
Penguin Books Canada Ltd, 10 Alcorn Avenue, Toronto, Ontario, Canada M4V 3B2
Penguin Books (N.Z.) Ltd, Cnr Rosedale and Airborne Roads,
Albany, Auckland 1310, New Zealand

Penguin Books Ltd, Registered Offices: Harmondsworth, Middlesex, England

Published by Dutton, a member of Penguin Putnam, Inc.

First printing, February 2003
1   3   5   7   9   10   8   6   4   2

REGISTERED TRADEMARK—MARCA REGISTRADA

LIBRARY OF CONGRESS CATALOGING-IN-PUBLICATION DATA

McFadden, Bernice L.
Loving Donovan / Bernice L. McFadden.
p. cm.
ISBN 0-525-94706-X (alk. paper)
1. African Americans—Fiction.   I. Title.

PS3563.C3622 L6 2003
813'.54—dc21   2002029812

Printed in the United States of America
Set in Galliard
Designed by Leonard Telesca

PUBLISHER'S NOTE
This book is a work of fiction. Names, characters, places, and incidents are either the product of the author's imagination or are used fictitiously, and any resemblance to actual persons, living or dead, business establishments, events, or locales is entirely coincidental.

For the men I've loved . . . and love still

Author's Note

Although this is a work of fiction, the emotions are real: pain, longing, love.

I am grateful to God, family and friends, who constantly lift me up. Their support has been tremendous, and their love overwhelming. Thank you . . . thank you . . . thank you.

To my daughter, R'yane Azsa, who knew the years would go by so quickly? You've grown into such a beautiful young lady. . . . I regret not having a dozen more. I love you so very much.

To my family at Dutton and the Vines agency, I am indebted and grateful.

Terry McMillan, your words of wisdom and friendship have been a source of great comfort for me. Thank you.

Pat Houser, thank you for your friendship and immense support.

To my readers, thank you for your continued support. Please keep the e-mails and letters coming; they are a constant source of joy for me.

All we need is love . . .

des·ti·ny (des-ti-nee) *n.* (*pl.* –**nies**) **1.** Fate considered as a power. **2.** That which happens to a person or thing, thought of as determined in advance by fate.

—Oxford American Dictionary, Oxford University Press, Inc. 1980

The love that lasts longest is the love that is never returned.

—W. Somerset Maugham, recalled on his death, December 16, 1965

Prologue

January 2003

When she recalls that period in her life, she likens it to a piece of the hard candy she'd often enjoyed as a child. Round, colorful, tangy, sweet on the outside, and bitter at the center.

Three years had come and gone, and since then Campbell had married a wonderful man from Kentucky, given birth to a son, moved to another part of the state, taken up pottery and yoga, leased a Mercedes, and purchased a beach house in Anguilla; her daughter, Macon, had made her a grandmother, and even with all of those life changes, her heart remained the same. Her heart remained with him.

She wished she could say that she thought of Donovan only when she heard Etta James belt out "At Last," or in the dead of night, midsummer, when it rained or snowed, or when the sun shone so brightly, it made the day too beautiful to behold.

He had been beautiful.

She wished she could say that her mind reached back to those times only when life was unbalanced and sad, but that would be an outright lie because she thought about that man even when she was happy and wrapped up tight in her husband's arms.

She thought about him when she held her newborn son to her breast, pulled her fingers through her hair, when she sighed, sneezed, breathed.

She thought about him.

She found him on her mind when she was surrounded by silence, engulfed by noise, when she sat, walked, stood in line at the grocery store.

Nikki Giovanni must have known someone similar, because she wrote about him in "Cancers (not necessarily a love poem)."

Damn! She thought about him.

And she asked herself, Would she leave? Would she leave everything she'd ever wanted and had finally gotten? Would she put all she had behind her if she opened her door one day and found him standing there, empty-handed but with a full heart?

Would she leave everything and everyone she had if he opened his mouth and simply said, "Hello. I'm sorry. I love you."

Would she go?

Shit, she believed she would.

Her

1973–1980

Age Eight

She can hear her mama in the kitchen talking loud to the walls, beating the pots, slapping her forehead with the palm of her hand, and wailing, Lord, why this man do the things he do to me!

Millie cries a little, small tears that cling to her cheeks like the tiny diamond earrings she swoons over in the JCPenney catalog. The same diamond earrings her husband, Fred, always promises to buy her, but never does.

When Campbell sees those tears, those wet diamonds, she thinks that they are pieces of her mama's fragile heart her daddy went and broke again.

Millie don't know why he act the way he do, say the things he say, and he don't seem to know either, 'cause when she ask him, he just shrugs his shoulders and says, "Baby, I'm sorry. I don't know why I spent the rent money, stayed out till dawn, had my hand on Viola Sampson's knee . . . Millie, baby, I just don't know."

He don't ever know, and he's always sorry.

Sorry is what he says all the time, and whenever Millie hears those words, she behaves as if it's the first time Fred's been ignorant and sorry, and she spit and cuss, slap at his head and punch at his chest, holler out how much she hates him, screams she wishes he was dead, and still climbs into bed with him at night.

Luscious says Millie married Fred because she felt she was getting old and was afraid she would end up a spinster, sitting out on the porch 'longside her, shooing flies and cuddling cats in her lap instead of babies.

"That's why your mama married your daddy. I don't think it was love, not the real kind that makes you walk with your back straight and your head high," she tells Campbell.

"I think I walk with my back straight, and I ain't in love," Campbell thinks to herself.

"Your mother ain't never been known to step in any dogshit or get the sole of her shoe messed up with gum. You know why?" Luscious asks, and cocks her head to one side.

Campbell shakes her head and waits.

" 'Cause your mama always walks slumped over with her head down."

Campbell rolls her eyes up and to the left and thinks about what Luscious says, and in her mind's eye she sees her mama walking to the supermarket, the Laundromat, and the butcher shop, head down, her eyes searching the sidewalk for something she won't talk about.

"Uh-huh," Campbell says, agreeing with Luscious.

Campbell asks Millie about what Luscious says; she asks, Is it true?

Millie tries to straighten the hump loving Fred done put on her back, and she twists her mouth up like she do on the day before the rent is due and it's long past seven and Fred still ain't home with his paycheck, and then she says, "Campbell," and her daughter's name is a long wind—and Millie takes another moment to fold her hands across her stomach before she continues.

"Campbell, your aunt Rita is old and feeble-minded and speak on things she don't know nothing about."

Millie doesn't refer to Luscious as Luscious; she calls her by her given name. Rita.

"I don't know where that Luscious nonsense came from!" Millie screams in frustration. "Her name is Rita Josephine Smith. That's what's on her birth certificate, baptismal record, and welfare check, and that's all I'll ever refer to her as!"

After Millie say what she got to say to Campbell, she sucks her teeth and waves her off with one hand while she reaches for the phone with the other and dials those seven digits that have belonged to Luscious for what seems to Campbell like forever.

She waits a few seconds, and Campbell don't hear her say hello or how ya doing or nothing; Millie just jumps right on Luscious and tells her to stop spreading lies and confusing her child's mind with foolishness.

There's no hiding her pain from her daughter, and Campbell stays close by while her mother weeps and wrings her hands in frustration until she can't take it anymore and settles herself down in her recliner. "Get me a beer, baby," she says to Campbell. "And my headache pills from the medicine cabinet."

Campbell is too young to know that aspirin don't come in prescription bottles and are not small yellow pills with the letter *V* stamped out of their center.

"Thank you, baby," Millie says, and gives Campbell a sad smile before she pops the pill on her tongue and takes a long swig of the beer.

Campbell will stay with Millie until her mother's eyes close and her head lolls on her neck. She'll spend those moments at the window, humming "Over the Rainbow" from *The Wizard of Oz*. It is a soothing tonic for her and Millie during tense times, and there are many of those.

Campbell finds herself at the window, her hands stroking the long emerald drapes, her eyes moving between her mother's sad face and the street below.

There is a lemon-colored sun resting peacefully in the pale summer sky. It's quiet except for the chirping of birds and the now and again blast of a car horn.

Not many people roam the streets on that sultry Sunday afternoon, and Campbell's eyes are growing heavy with boredom when the *click-click* sounds of a woman's heel against the pavement—faint at first, and then swelling—pique her interest.

Campbell leans a bit over the windowsill, and her eyes fall on auburn hair and the mocha-colored shoulders of a woman who has a small pink suitcase clutched in one hand while her free hand, balled into a tight fist, punches at the air with every fourth step she takes.

She's wearing open-toed, strapless baby-blue clogs that whack at her heels as she speeds along. Campbell winces at the sound but notes the fresh pedicure and wonders why Millie doesn't take that sort of time with herself.

Before the woman reaches the corner, Campbell has the urge to call out to her. For some reason she needs to see her face, needs to see the lines in her forehead and maybe the set of her mouth and color of her eyes.

But she's only eight years old, and that would be out of place, and Millie would call her mannish and grown and probably twist her ear or pop her upside her head.

So she bites her lip against the urge, and the woman disappears around the corner taking the punching hand and the clicking whacking sounds with her.

Millie begins to snore, and Campbell turns to look at her. She observes the mussed hair and the salty tracks her tears have abandoned on her cheeks. Campbell thinks that it is a shame, a downright shame. But those are Luscious's words, not hers.

Campbell retires to her bedroom and pulls her journal from its hiding place beneath her bed, opens it to a clean page, marking her name, age, and date at the top, and beginning with

Ain't no man ever going to make me cry, make me talk to the walls and wail out to the Lord.

Ain't no man ever going to break my heart.

Age Ten

As far back as Campbell could remember, there were no flowers in the courtyards of the Brookline housing projects. No flowers, but plenty of beer bottles, candy wrappers, and other pieces of debris that people saw fit to toss over the chain-link fences.

Each spring, Housing came through to repaint and repair the benches that had been vandalized during the year, sloshing green paint over the nicknames, gang tags, and declarations of love that had been scrawled there with spray paint and Magic Marker.

The halls of Brookline Projects smelled like piss, reefer, and—according to Luscious—Maria Santos's nasty ass.

She said this because she had heard Maria screwing in the stairwell a number of times, had heard her scream, *"Ay, Papi!"* over and over again, and had seen the discarded condoms on the steps, and Luscious said the scent Maria left behind was ungodly.

The intercom system in the Brookline projects was always

broken, that and the locks on the doors. Housing gave up on repairing those things, leaving its residents vulnerable to whoever wanted in. They concentrated instead on installing wire encasements over the light fixtures to keep vandals from breaking the bulbs only, making the residents easy targets in the darkness.

They just became easy targets in the light.

Most apartments were mice- and roach-infested, and hot water was something you prayed for before you turned on the shower.

When people moved, Brookline residents ran to their windows, gathered on the benches, or balanced their behinds on the chain-link fences to watch the tattered sofas, mismatched kitchen chairs, color television, bookshelves, wall units, and various other pieces of furniture the family had accumulated over the years loaded into the borrowed van, rented U-Haul, or box-shaped delivery truck Juan Miguel had bought from a junkman on Euclid Avenue for five hundred dollars two years earlier. The red letters on the left side of the truck still screamed WONDER BREAD, glowing through the cheap white paint he'd smeared across it last spring.

Luscious would watch from the bench that sat closest to the doorway. The one she'd claimed as her own so many years ago. It was her throne, and in warm weather she could be found there most of the day and well into the night.

She was the queen of 256 Stanley Avenue, Brookline Projects.

Everyone knew Luscious, and Luscious knew everyone.

She'd arrived there from Detroit in 1953. Back then, the apartments were still filled with white people, the courtyards with colorful blooms that lasted from April straight through to October.

The benches unmarked, well-lit hallways, working elevators, and clean stairwells.

Neighbors bidding you hello or good night, and even asking about that ailing family member they'd heard about.

Back then, Luscious was hefty but still considered a good-looking woman. Green-eyed and honey-colored with soft wavy hair that rested on her shoulders.

Like Brookline Projects, Luscious would change, and her beauty would become a shadow of what it once was. Her weight would bloom from two hundred to four, and her skin would hang in folds, her beauty retreating into the creases of her flesh, and Luscious would look every bit the hog people began to refer to her as.

In 1975, on Campbell's moving day, Luscious sits and watches over the broken pavement on a blemished bench beside Campbell and Campbell's closest friends: Pat, Anita, Porsche, and Laverna.

The girls have been together since nursery school, and they would be together in one form or another throughout their adult lives, but on that sweltering July day, Campbell was fragmenting their circle, leaving them behind and moving what seemed to them miles away—to another part of Brooklyn.

Luscious nudges Campbell's waist and winks at the girls. "So will you come and visit us? Or will you forget all about us once you're gone?" she asks.

The girls look at Campbell expectantly.

"Uh-huh," Campbell replies, and slurps up the last bit of soda from the can. "Y'all gonna come and visit me?" Campbell poses the same question.

"Hmmm, maybe," Luscious says nonchalantly, and starts to examine the chipped pink polish on her fingernails while the girls rapidly nod their heads.

Luscious's response forces the loose smile on Campbell's face to fall away. The girls twist their mouths and give each other the "I told you she was mean" look.

"Maybe?" Campbell questions, and her bottom lip drops in disappointment.

The corners of Luscious's mouth tremble, and a light not often seen dances in her eyes, and Campbell knows she's kidding and happily exclaims, "Yeah, you will!" and all of them break down with laughter.

More furniture sails past them, and then the black Hefty bags heavy with clothes and shoes.

"No, we don't need any help, Campbell," Millie says sarcastically as she makes her hundredth trip past them. "Yours neither, Rita," she slings at Luscious.

"Good thing for you!" Luscious yells back at Millie. "Your mama always gotta be starting with someone," Luscious says to Campbell, and rolls her eyes.

"Here, Campbell, go on over to the store, and get me a bag of potato chips, a Pepsi cola, and some Now and Laters," she says, and stuffs a dollar into her hand.

The girls give Luscious a quick look and then drop their eyes to their sneakers. Luscious considers them for a moment and then pulls another dollar from her bosom. "Get your little friends something, too."

They move into a brownstone on Bainbridge Street in the Bedford-Stuyvesant section of Brooklyn. The house is old and leans to one side, but Millie don't seem to mind that or the fact that all three fireplaces are sealed.

"They don't even work no more," Fred says. But Millie doesn't care; she likes them, working or not. She's content with just looking at them and admiring the intricately carved wooden mantels. Those mantels will help to occupy her thoughts, and she can forget that Fred cheats and hardly ever reaches for her anymore at night.

She will keep those mantels dust free and glowing and won't even complain when Fred measures the floors for wall-to-wall carpeting. "It'll save on the heating bill," he says.

Campbell waves bye-bye to the beautiful design in the wood floors and looks up at the twelve-foot-high ceilings and wonders about what's living in the cobwebs that occupy all the corners above her head and if her new room is far enough away to block out the sound of her mother's weeping.

When they purchased the house, they inherited the tenant, Clyde Walker, a squat man with red-brown skin and bulging eyes.

Fred advised him that he would have to go up on his rent by fifteen dollars.

"Well, I ain't about to pay no more than I been paying. Been paying too much already. Floors squeak, pipes leak, had pneumonia every winter I been here. Drafty, oil burner work when it want to. Cold water freezing, hot water cold. I ain't paying no more than I been paying."

"So I guess you'll be leaving, then," Fred said real quiet-like before reaching into the breast pocket of his shirt and pulling out his pack of Winstons.

"Guess so." Clyde Walker said just as quietly, and closed his door.

A week later he was gone.

Campbell was more than happy for that. She had encountered him a few times sitting out on the front stoop, his back resting against the step, his hands working at something deep inside the pockets of his pants, his mouth toiling away at the red-and-white-striped peppermints he constantly sucked on.

"Hello, pretty girl," he would say, but his words were oil slick, and something about the sound of his voice and the way he looked at her made Campbell's skin crawl.

Yes, she was more than happy to see him lumbering down the sidewalk, suitcase in one hand, overcoat in the other, good-bye and so long sailing over his shoulder.

Good riddance!

Two weeks after that, Clarence Simon rang the bell and inquired about the sign Millie had placed in the front window. APARTMENT FOR RENT.

Millie showed it to him, moving through the small space, pointing out things like the women that showed the prizes on *The Price Is Right*: "And here we have . . ." "The bathroom is over to the left. . . ." "The rug was just shampooed and the windows cleaned. . . ." She spoke softly as she glided through the house with her practiced smile. "Already furnished, but still plenty of room for anything you might have," she said as she admired Clarence's long lean body and dark, neat suit.

"Two hundred a month, including light and gas," she said, and her eyes dropped to his well-manicured nails and the black snakeskin briefcase with the gold embossed letters that gleamed right below the handle.

"This is fine." Clarence said as he counted out one month's rent and one month's security.

He moved in the following Saturday, him and his friend.

Clarence Simon and Awed Johnson. Roommates.

Fred peeked through the curtains again. "He tell you he was going to share the place with someone?"

Millie wrung her hands nervously and paced at her husband's heels. "No, but I—"

"Did you even ask?"

"No, I didn't think to—"

"Shit, Millie, can't you even handle business right?"

Fred never took his eyes off Clarence and Awed. He stayed at that window until every last box, suitcase, and lamp was off the sidewalk and in his house.

"Two men. I don't know," Fred said when he finally turned around to look at his wife.

Clarence's friend—his roommate, Awed—was barely five feet tall, with midnight skin and a broad chest. Dagger tattoos dripping blood graced his left and right biceps. A shag of hair hung at his chin, and he would plait it into four braids, clasping the ends with multicolored rubber bands.

Campbell thought he was handsome, in a jailhouse sort of way, even with the fishhook scar that started at the top of his right ear and ended in a curve just above his cheekbone.

"You make sure you stay away from him. Both of them," Fred warned Campbell before throwing Millie a nasty look. "They mess up one time, and they're on the street," he said.

Awed claimed to work construction, but he seemed to be home more often than he was at work. From what Campbell could tell, he spent most of his days chain-smoking, drinking beer, and blasting his Rick James albums.

You could hear everything through the heating vents. Everything.

Clarence, on the other hand, toiled away as a paralegal for a number of prestigious downtown law firms.

"Well, you know at Lieberman, Hertz, and Fitz, we don't have to . . ." "At Lieberman, Katz, and Jacobson, we always . . ." "I may have to look for another job because Lieb, Howard, and Cole . . ."

Clarence changed jobs regularly. Six times in the first three months they'd known him.

"Mrs. Loring. Mrs. L.—Helllooooooo!" he'd sung through the door one day. "I picked you up a little something. Just a little gift you know, to celebrate . . . celebrate the house and well . . . you've been such great landlords. A little housewarming-slash-appreciation gift, I guess." Clarence had a tendency to babble. He shoved a small red-and-white-striped box at Millie.

"Oh," she exclaimed as she looked down at the words JU-NIOR'S WORLD'S MOST FABULOUS CHEESECAKE.

"Oh," she said again, and then smiled with delight. "You really shouldn't have gone to so much—"

"Oh, it was no trouble at all. It's a strawberry cheesecake, my favorite. My, do you like cheesecake? Strawberries? Stupid, stupid me, I really should have checked with you first, shouldn't I? I mean, you could hate cheesecake—be allergic to strawberries, even. I had a friend that was allergic to strawberries; he would just swell up like a big red ball whenever he had one. How could anyone be allergic to a little ol' strawberry? I mean, they are the sweetest things. Now blackberries, yuck! I hate those with a passion. I could understand a person's body breaking out in hives after having one of those things, although some say the blacker the berry the sweeter the—oh, look at me going on and on."

Clarence finally took a breath, and Millie took one right along with him. Campbell, who had been listening from the kitchen just giggled to herself.

"I love strawberries and cheesecake. Thank you so much," Millie said, and another warm smile spread across her face.

"You're welcomed. Very, very welcomed." Clarence said, and surprisingly turned and walked upstairs without another word.

"Yeah, he's got plenty of sugar in his tank," Fred commented afterwards as he grabbed a glass from the cabinet.

"Oh, Fred. Some men are just a little feminine—it don't mean he's gay."

"Oh, he's a faggot all right," Fred said as he held the glass up to the light to examine it.

"Fred!" Millie screamed, and turned on him.

"What?" He gave her dumbfounded look.

"That word, it's disgusting."

"What word, *faggot?*"

Millie went rigid. "Yes."

"Well, that's what he is, Millie. I'm just calling it the way I see it."

"Can't you just say *gay* like the rest of the world?"

"I don't know anybody who says *gay*, Millie. What world do you live in?"

"Stop it," Millie said, and shook her head.

Well, it was becoming quite evident to Campbell that Clarence did have a little sugar in his tank.

The more comfortable he became with them, the more melodious his voice grew, the more expressive his hands became as he used them to pilot him through conversations. Campbell thought of them, his hands, as pigeons during their morning flights over her house, diving and climbing, their movements sensuous and erratic all at once.

Fred rarely stayed to listen to Clarence's drawn-out, overwrought stories, but Millie and Campbell quietly, politely took in every word he had to say.

If Clarence was gay, then Awed was something else, but at that tender age, Campbell didn't know what the proper term should be.

It seemed that Awed liked women, too, liked them enough to bring them home when Clarence was at work, bring them home and do to them what he did to Clarence on nights Clarence came home with a case of beer or a fifth of Scotch.

Somehow Campbell felt that Awed didn't touch him in that way on evenings when Clarence came home empty-handed.

One day, as Campbell sat at the kitchen table trying to concentrate on a particular history problem, a steady knocking started beneath her. She was used to the sound, accustomed to hearing it on nights when the house was quiet and she was supposed to be asleep.

On those nights, Millie would pull herself out of bed and turn the television on to drown out the sound of Clarence and Awed's lovemaking. If Fred happened to be home, he would shake his head in disgust, grab his bathrobe, and step outside to have a cigarette or take a walk.

It was always over quickly, just as Fred flicked the glowing butt of his Winston out into the street or rounded the corner that happened to have a working pay phone.

But on that day, the sun still high in the sky and schoolchildren playing hopscotch on the street, the knocking sound was annoying, and Campbell thought it inappropriate for that time of day.

She slammed her pencil down on the table and pressed her hands over her ears until curiosity overwhelmed her and she scurried from the chair and down to the floor to press her ear to the vent.

She heard a woman's soft giggle and then Awed's voice, thick and guttural, "Whose pussy is this, bitch!" and the thumping sounds became louder, faster.

"Yours! Yours!" the woman screamed.

Campbell's eyes bulged.

"Whose, whose!"

"A-a-aweeeeeeeeed!"

Campbell remained at the vent, alternating ears, ignoring the pain the beige and white linoleum was causing on her soft knees. She was mesmerized with the lewd call-and-response game Awed and his lady friend played.

"Whose, whose, whose!"

"Aweeeeeeeeeed!"

Millie called from work, just as she did every day at 4 P.M.

"Hello?" Campbell answered breathlessly, the sudden ringing of the phone catching her off guard and making her feel guilty.

"What you doing?" Millie asked suspiciously. "Who's there?"

"No one—I was in the bathroom."

"Uh-huh."

Millie announced that she would be detained at least another hour and said for Campbell to remove the frozen chicken parts that she planned to fry for dinner that night.

"Is your father home?" she asked as an afterthought, but Campbell knew that Millie had wanted to ask that question at the very beginning of the conversation.

"No." She sighed, her eyes glued to the vent, her ears straining to hear what she was missing.

Fred had not come home from work yet. He worked the midnight-to-eight shift for sanitation and should have been home by ten o'clock that morning, but it was just past four, and he'd still not arrived.

Millie was quiet for a moment and then offered a quick goodbye before slamming the receiver down in its cradle.

Her mother's orders forgotten, Campbell rushed back to the vent. Just as she was getting herself situated, the front door swung open, and Clarence whisked in, hands laden with shopping bags.

"Hello, princess Campbell!" he sang before gliding down the stairs to his apartment.

"Hey," she yelled back.

She'd barely been able to get to her feet before he'd breezed past the door. If it had been closed, like it was supposed to be, she wouldn't have had to move at all, but she'd gotten so used to it being open when her parents were home and had taken to doing the same.

She could hear Clarence jiggling the lock, could hear the keys clinking together as Clarence became more and more frustrated. He breathed and then sucked his teeth before knocking on the door; he knocked softly at first and then called to Awed through the door.

"Awed . . . Awed, you've got the double lock on. You know I don't have a key for that. Awed?"

Awed's feet hit the floor; quick shuffling sounds followed as he and whatever woman he had there tried desperately to locate their clothing.

"Awed!" Clarence's voice was shrill. He'd heard the rustling, shuffling sounds, too. "Awed, you open this door right this minute. Right this goddamn minute!"

Clarence banged on the door now, his shouts climbing to the screams of a frantic woman.

Campbell wondered if she should call the police, Millie, or Luscious, but she couldn't move; she was glued to the vent.

There was an endless instant of silence that was so intense she could hear the insistent *tick-tick-tick* of the pumpkin clock that sat on the wall above the refrigerator.

She held her breath and waited.

"Gimme a damn minute," Awed's voice finally came.

The door slowly opened, and Clarence was met with a dusky blackness that was weighed down with the scent of cigarettes, beer, and sex.

Awed, who was wearing just a pair of red-and-white-striped boxer shorts, stood with his arms folded across his chest. The sight of him, half-naked with that nonchalant look on his face, almost undid Clarence, but he quickly composed himself and screamed, "Oh, no, you didn't bring some bitch up in here!" Clarence pushed past Awed and stormed into the apartment. "Where is she! Where is that skank!"

Awed just snorted, scratched his balls, and calmly followed Clarence inside.

There was a scream. Campbell couldn't tell if it was the woman or Clarence. A crashing sound followed and then another scream.

"Oh, bitch, you done did it now!" Clarence screeched before a half-dressed female, whom Campbell recognized as the token booth clerk from the Ralph Avenue train station, came running out.

Her jeans were on, but only halfway up her hips, leaving quite a bit of her naked behind exposed.

She took the stairs two at a time, her face a canvas of terror. Clarence was on her heels, his long fingers grasping for the shoulder-length synthetic hair that flared out behind her like a woolen cape.

Campbell was in the hallway by then. The woman made it through the front door, but only because Clarence lost his footing when he slipped on the throw rug that Millie had laid out in the hallway for days when the rain fell and shoe bottoms were damp and muddy.

What followed was horrible, Clarence pacing the hallway, his hands balled into tight fists, him screaming and crying, cussing at the top of his lungs.

Awed just watched him, a thin smirk painted across his face. When he'd heard enough and seen enough, he waved his hand at Clarence, blew some air from between his lips, turned, shot Campbell an even look, and descended the stairs to his apartment—and quietly closed the door.

Clarence let out a wounded sound and crumpled to the floor. He pulled his knees up to his chest and began sobbing uncontrollably.

Campbell's heart was racing. She'd never seen a man cry before, none except for the drunks in Brookline Projects. But this was different; this was out-and-out sobbing that she'd seen only from women at funerals.

Campbell snatched a napkin from the holder on the kitchen table and carefully approached Clarence, not sure what to do and finally just sort of stuffing the napkin in between Clarence's clenched hands.

"Th-thank you, princess," he said as he began dabbing the corner of his eyes with it. "I'm so sorry you had to be here for this madness," he said, and forced a shaky smile. "Awed is just a piece of shit," he said, and a fresh stream of tears poured down his face. "A bastard," he added, and then wiped at his face again.

"Well, I suppose it's all out in the open now, huh, princess?" he mumbled as he stood up and brushed at the creases in his pants leg.

Campbell didn't know what Clarence was referring to, the part about Awed being unfaithful or that he was a piece of shit.

She looked at Clarence and then down at her feet. "Uhm," she uttered, and bit her bottom lip.

"Well, it's not that I'm ashamed of being gay, it's just that not everybody understands or accepts it, you know what I mean, princess?" Clarence said.

"Oh," she said, understanding now. "Oh, uh-huh." She raised her eyes to meet his.

"Well, so now you know," Clarence said, and shrugged his shoulders before wiping at his eyes again. "Now you know, and I suppose you'll run and tell everybody you know."

"No, I won't," she said a little too quickly, and felt like maybe she should cross her heart and swear to God, but she just shook her head for emphasis.

Clarence ran his hands over his hair and cleared his throat. "Well, good. It's nobody's business but mine and that piece of shit downstairs."

He smiled at her, but the sadness and the hurt were still swimming in his eyes.

"Men ain't shit. You'll find that out soon enough, princess." Clarence straightened his shoulders. "Don't ever fall in love; it'll kick you in your ass every time," he said, and turned and walked down the stairs.

Campbell watched him walk away, defeated.

She remained there in the hallway for some time, chewing on her already chewed-away fingernails, waiting for the second round of anger, but it never came.

Late that night, as Johnny Carson bade his audience good night on Fred and Millie's nineteen-inch Zenith, Clarence's breathless "I love you's" stole through the vents, and Millie hugged herself, wishing Fred was lying inside her, uttering the same.

Age Thirteen

Campbell's hips protrude, and her behind does much of the same. She's interested in lip gloss, perfume, fancy hair clips, and fashion magazines now.

Millie notices her daughter's approaching womanhood, like one detects something from the corner of one's eye when the mind is concentrating on other things. A glint of gold that turns to brass. Campbell should be her main concern, but Fred is all that she can think of.

Campbell is a young lady now, Millie explains to her. She needs to remember to keep her legs closed and crossed at the ankle, not at the thigh.

She spews other decrees, regulations, and requirements that Campbell tries hard to remember and hang on to, but they're swept away with the April breeze when Trevor Barzey walks up to her one day and says hello.

Trevor Barzey, a brown-skinned, thick-lipped, slanty-eyed

brother from Jamaica, lives on the seventh floor of 256 Stanley Avenue.

Rumor has it that he has children from various girls Campbell went to preschool with, those and the twins he fathered on Eighty-sixth Street with a woman old enough to be his mother. "I've seen them," her friend Pat said. "They have his eyes."

He'd been with most of the girls in the neighborhood.

The fast-talking ones that wore summer hot pants straight through October. The ones that lined their eyes and glossed their lips.

He'd had some parochial school girls, the nondenominational Sunday-go-to-meeting girls, and the ones that scored high in algebra and history.

He'd had all of them, so when he turned his attention to Campbell, she was flattered.

Trevor talked a lot about the white man, the revolution that wouldn't be televised, and the fact that his father had been a Black Panther.

Luscious told her that she'd known Trevor's father, and warned her niece that owning a black beret and dark shades did not a Black Panther make.

In the beginning, it's just conversation; he confronts her when she returns to Stanley Avenue to visit her friends and Luscious. He asks about her parents first and then school. His eyes move over her high firm breasts that strain against the pink of her sweater and then drop to her hips and shapely thighs.

"You all grown up and stuff now." Trevor speaks from the side of his mouth as his eyes continue to travel Campbell's body.

They begin to meet like that every Sunday, and Campbell finds herself looking forward to seeing Trevor, him touching her wrist and sometimes fingering her hair.

By May, they're spending time in the hallway, him stealing

kisses from her before she steps on to the elevator that brings her up to Luscious's apartment.

In June they're up on the top floor, in the stairwell that leads to the roof. Campbell's pressed up against the wall, the cold cinder blocks against her back, wondering about how she will smell after she leaves him because people piss against those walls.

Somewhere below the steady buzzing sound of the overhead fluorescents, she hears the heavy zipper of Trevor's Lee jeans come undone.

Campbell slides her hands down to his waist and looks over his shoulder at the wall and then down to the floor and the puddle of grape soda someone has spilled there, looking everywhere except down at his crotch.

He grabs hold of her hand and guides it between them, places it . . . down there. She feels it, and it feels hard. Her breath catches in her throat, and she concentrates harder on the purple puddle of soda.

He presses against her and forces his penis to slide between the curled fingers of her damp palm, and then he slips his hand beneath her sweatshirt, the white one that has ANGEL spelled across it in bright pink letters.

Campbell holds on to his penis, not sure exactly what she should do, her mind wandering on the Italian bread Fred sends her to buy at the grocery store. She holds his penis like the Italian bread, like she's standing on line waiting to pay.

He begins moving faster and faster, and she can hear him moaning and whispering things in her ear that she does not understand. But her grip is tighter now, and she closes her eyes against the purple soda and pissy beige cinder-block walls.

"Ohhhh," he moans, and it echoes through the halls, and Campbell's eyes fly open again—and finally she looks down at his penis and understands immediately why they call it a dick.

It's so swollen that she thinks it's going to explode, so she squeezes down hard on it, tries to crush away the wavy-looking veins that are pushing through the skin. She squeezes down hard, and he makes that sound again that echoes through the halls and gets her insides boiling.

His whole body is pushing and pulling, and his hands have forgotten about her titties and are now flat against the wall, trying to push the wall down. "I—I—I—"

He's trying to say something, so she squeezes again because maybe his words are caught inside his dick.

"Shit!" he yells, and suddenly her hands are wet.

"Shit," he whispers, breathless this time, and she realizes that her hands are wet and sticky.

He falls against her for a moment and then rolls off to the side and onto the wall.

"Damn," he mutters as he wipes his dick off with the end of his T-shirt.

She looks down at it again. It's not long, hard, or throbbing anymore. It's drawn up, shriveled and glistening like the dwarf pickles that float in the jar on the counter at the corner store.

Campbell wonders if this is what love is.

Age Fourteen

She notices them because the child, a girl with big eyes and small lips, smiles all the time, while the mother—petite, dark skinned, with the same wee lips—frowns. In the summer, Campbell sees them standing near the corner to the west of the house, or across the street by the wall where someone has written JESUS SAVES. Other times, just before the sun dips, they move close to the bodega.

She notices them because the child, no more than two years old, is so well behaved, content as long as one hand is clutching her doll and the other is wrapped tightly in her mother's hand.

When the rain falls, they huddle in the vestibule of the building that is diagonal to Campbell's brownstone, the child waving hello and good-bye to the residents who move in and out of the doorways. Smiling, always smiling.

The mother makes way, but her frown is constant, and her

eyes never leave Campbell's stoop for more than a few seconds at a time.

When autumn arrives, she notices them because they are more conspicuous in their white winter coats with faux fur collars the color of red wine.

Millie notices them, too. Not at first, not in the summer or in the early days of September, but they catch her eye during mid-October, when the leaves are burnt orange and brilliant yellow.

They are on the corner, beneath the tree, leaves falling around them like rain, and Millie's pace slows so that she can get a good look at the little girl with the crimson collar.

"So cute," Millie says, and then looks up at the woman.

When their eyes meet, Millie's shoulders stiffen, and her mouth drops and then snaps tightly shut before she moves on, her pace fast, her body trembling.

The woman's eyes are sparkling, and for the first time her frown has turned upright into a smile.

Once in the house, Millie smokes, cusses, and polishes the mantels in between making trips to the windows, snatching the curtains aside, and swinging her eyes up and down the block looking for the woman, the child, and her husband.

Sometimes she looks so hard that she bumps her head against the glass and, disgusted, she sucks her teeth, mutters a curse word, and then snatches the front door open and steps out onto the stoop.

But her eyes just fall on neighbors and strangers making their way home from work.

When Fred finally comes through the door, that woman's autumn leaves are swirling at his feet, and his face looks like a cozy blanket; his eyes are soft and full like pillows. Millie knows that look; she has been acquainted with it for little more than fourteen years. That is his after-lovemaking look.

The look on his face, the swirling leaves at his feet, and the memory of the frowning woman send her into a rage, and she's in his face before he can complain about the house stinking of Pledge and Merit cigarettes, because all Millie has been doing since she walked through the door is smoking and polishing the mantels and mumbling over and over, "That bastard, that no-good bastard."

Her hands are balled into tight knots that turn her skin red at the knuckles, and her shoulders are hunched up close to her neck. Campbell's stomach growls, but she won't even fix her mouth to ask about dinner, and she goes into the kitchen to make a peanut butter and jelly sandwich.

"Millie," he starts, but Millie hauls off and slaps him across his face before he can finish.

"Woman, are you crazy!" Fred screams as he stumbles backwards from the blow.

"Yeah, Niggah, crazy for marrying your sorry ass!" Millie screams back.

Campbell jumps up, and the plate and sandwich go crashing to the floor.

Fred is just standing there in shock, a hand cradling his cheek while Millie starts talking so fast that the only words they grab on to are "Whore" and "No respect."

Fred tosses back, "You crazy" and "Bellevue."

Millie is through with throwing words, so she kicks off her slippers and throws those; she does the same with the brown-and-tan Mary Janes that sit in the corner, snatches up the lamp from the end table, and finally yanks off her wedding ring. Fred ducks and dodges each object, and they all end up on the floor behind him.

"You crazy, woman," is all he says before walking up the stairs and into their bedroom.

Millie doesn't follow; she just grabs up her dust cloth and Pledge and begins polishing the mantels again.

When the letters start coming, plain white envelopes with FRED typed neatly across the front, Millie doesn't know what to make of them.

She won't open them. Opening them would mean facing the truth completely, and she's not ready to do that, so she places them on the kitchen table, or on the refrigerator door, behind the magnet that says CANCUN.

"You told me it was over," she whispers to him when Campbell has gone upstairs or into the living room to watch television.

"It is," Fred says in a bored voice.

"Then what the hell is this, huh?" She points at the envelope.

"How would I know? I haven't opened it."

"Then open it," she hisses.

"When I get ready," Fred says before snatching up the envelope, stuffing it into his pocket, and walking out the back door.

She watches him from the window, out in the cold, cigarette hanging from his lips, hands shaking as he works at opening the envelope.

The wind snatches at the letter, but Fred holds on tight until he's read every word, and then he refolds it, reaches in his pocket for his lighter, and lets the blue-and-yellow flame have its way with it.

Millie's tears come then, and so does the throbbing at her temples. She's out of pills, and there's only one beer left in the fridge, so she snatches it from its shelf and eases herself down at the kitchen table, propping her feet up in the chair, lighting a cigarette, and popping the tab from the can.

Her mind will wander to her mantels, but mostly to the wrong turn she took fourteen years ago that landed her here.

There is no love inside apartment 4G, 256 Stanley Avenue. Only silence and brooding since they'd left Detroit on the heels of their mother's death in 1953.

There is no love in that place, and Luscious doesn't invite any in, especially the love that walks on two legs and arrives with flowers, calling her beautiful and trying to convince her that she was in need of a good man, leaning in close and whispering that they would be sweet together. Sweet.

Luscious just scoffs and laughs at them, not one of those wide-mouthed, tilt-your-head-back-on-your-neck types of laugh that would reveal the cotton candy pink of her tongue and the rotting centers of her molars. If she'd laughed like that for them, they would see and know without her ever having to tell them that all the sweetness she'd had in her life came from the powdered coating of doughnuts and the sugary syrup of cola.

No love, just Luscious working double shifts at the factory, coming home dog-tired and evil, not sharing a word with Millie unless it was to scold her or warn her against the evil of men.

No love and no tenderness, and so Millie looks for those things from her aunts and uncles on Flatbush Avenue; she looks for it from her teachers and the crossing guard who smiles at her in the mornings when she's on her way to school. When she's older, she looks for it from boys who want to touch her beneath her skirt and stick their tongues in her mouth, and later, when Luscious finally loosens the reins she has on Millie, she looks for it from the men who whisper words that make her blush before they take her in their arms and lie to her about love.

Millie has had three heartbreaks by the time she finally notices Fred in the fall of '64.

She sees him at the bus stop; he's small, but stretches his five-foot-five frame a whole two inches taller when their eyes finally meet.

His ring finger absent of a ring, she smiles her brightest smile and asks God to please, please let him be the one.

They date for three months before she gives herself to him.

His touch is sobering and does not spring the wild madness that her last lover's touch did. Millie supposes that it's a good thing, a safe thing.

She accepts him between her legs on a day she has marked off in red on her calendar, a day that is one of five that is possible for her to conceive on, because she's studied Fred, his movements and philosophies on family, and what makes a man a man, and she's confident that when she meets him for lunch a month later and whispers in his ear that she's with child, he will do the right thing, the responsible thing.

The tuna fish and rye gets caught in his throat, and he looks over Millie's shoulder and past the counter into the chrome of the industrial-size coffee machine; he catches sight of his freedom skipping off into the sunset before suggesting that they do the right thing, the responsible thing, and marry.

The wedding is small.

They wed in March at Our Lady of Grace, a tiny old church whose pews are splintered and whose stained glass windows are patched with cardboard and masking tape, which does little to keep out the winter cold, so no one removes their coats and they curse themselves for leaving their gloves in their cars.

They take the vacant apartment below Luscious, and Millie busies herself with her new home, husband, and impending arrival. Campbell comes just six months later, and soon after that Fred begins to change.

There are late nights and the lingering scent of perfume clinging to his shirt collar. In his pockets there are bits of paper, some with numbers, and others with just a name, a place, and a time.

Millie calls the numbers, shows up at the addresses, and sometimes questions the women who are there.

Campbell is always with her. A reminder for Fred and the belief in family he once held. Millie bundles up her child in the yellow snowsuit and sets her down in her carriage before stuffing a warm bottle in her purse and setting out to look for her husband. *Her husband.*

Most times she finds him, his head bad from drinking, his hand resting on an exposed thigh or head resting against a delicate shoulder. A shouting match follows, sometimes things are thrown, once blood was drawn.

Fred always ends up going home with her, Millie cussing all the way, reminding him that he is her husband. *Her husband.*

When Luscious sees Millie looking haggard, her mind occupied, she asks, "Things okay?"

"Just fine," Millie lies.

Luscious knows otherwise. She hears the yelling, the screaming, accusations being thrown around like baseballs and then the slamming of doors, breaking of glasses, and sometimes the loud thuds on the walls when Fred has had enough and stops using his mouth and begins using his hands.

Luscious just shakes her head. She'd told her that she would regret the day and mourn the hour she ever got married, but a husband was a prize Millie thought she had to have, like a gorgeous pair of shoes or proper purse.

"That's good," Luscious replies before popping a handful of jelly beans in her mouth.

Millie just forces a smile. She will make her marriage work and prove Luscious wrong about men and love and commitment.

She will, even if it kills her.

Age Fifteen

The apartment was empty when they arrived. Trevor snatched a white piece of paper from the door that said NOTICE OF EVICTION across the top before grabbing her arm and tugging her over the threshold.

It was a small one-bedroom, like Luscious's place, except the floors were covered in cranberry shag, and the walls were painted white instead of the standard housing-issued egg cream. There were framed pictures of Trevor's father placed here and there on every wall. "What's his name?" Campbell asked. "Ray Vaughn," Trevor replied, and pushed his chest out when he said it.

Ray Vaughn posing on one knee, bare chest, tight jeans, dark shades, making the peace sign with his fingers. Ray Vaughn posed somewhere in a park, green army fatigues, black beret, and dark shades, cradling an AK-47 in his arms.

Ray Vaughn with some other men in a tight space with bunk

beds, magazine cutouts of naked women pasted on the wall behind them. This time he didn't wear the dark shades, and there
was something missing from his eyes, something lost years before
the judge banged down his gavel and sentenced him to life.

The apartment was filled with the same scent that lingers in
the stairwells when the housing patrol takes a night off and there
is no one available to chase away the reefer-smoking hoodlums.

Trevor's bed is a twin rollaway folded away neatly in the corner of the living room beside the black leather sofa. Trevor will
pull that bed from its corner and ask Campbell if she might like
to sit down.

Later, Campbell will focus on the flowered sheet that covers
the mattress, that and the brown metal rail of the bed. She fo-
cuses on those things hard, and for as long as she can, until he
pushes her legs apart and is able to get his fingers all the way
down between her legs and then up inside her.

Her eyes let go, and her neck goes weak, and the only strength
she has left in her body must be in her arms because she embraces
him. He wants to put something else inside her. He needs to put
something else inside her, he says.

"Please," he coaxes. "C'mon," he begs.

She can stay only an hour at a time; anything over that and
Luscious will place a call back to the house to find out what time
she left—any more than that and she can't explain where the
time has gone, and Millie will cut out the visits altogether.

She shakes her head, pushes his hand away, and sits up. Trevor
groans in frustration before getting up and disappearing down
the hall and into his mother's bedroom. When he comes back,
he's holding a lit joint between his lips.

"You ever done this?" he asks before he takes a hit and
holds it in.

Campbell shakes her head again.

Trevor moves beside her now, puffing and blowing smoke in Campbell's face. "You want to try it?"

She thinks about the friends who have. The ones who tease her sometimes and call her square, and she shakes her head. Slowly this time, like she might want to but needs a little push.

"Just take one hit. Just to see how it feels," he says.

She coughs the first few times, but by the sixth pull, she is able to hold it in, and her body becomes heavy, but her head light.

Campbell would remember laughing, laughing so much that her sides began to ache, and she fell over and onto the black leather couch. She could see Trevor grinning above her, the fold-away twin bed unfolded and resting in the center of the room.

She didn't know how much time had passed, but when the laughter finally settles into giggles and the giggles leave her with just a twitching mouth, she's naked and spread out on the bed, and Trevor is already on top of her, pushing up inside her.

"I'm a virgin," she whimpers into his neck.

"I know. I know." He moans and kisses her cheek.

Campbell can hear the radiators whistling and knocking, the windows blanketed in steam, but her body is cold, convulsing against the chill.

She thought she must have been screaming, because his hand is over her mouth, his mouth whispering "Shhhhh, baby, shhhhh," in her ear.

There is pressure building up inside her, moving up above her waist and into her chest until it's all in her shoulders and trapped in her head. Campbell thinks that if she could scream—if she could scream, she could get some release, but he won't remove his hand.

Campbell hears the song in her head, her theme song, climbing, climbing, "Somewhere over the rainbow . . ."

Suddenly, everything around her is too loud, the singing voice in her head, Trevor's breathing and groaning. She wants it all to stop, wants everything to end, and she manages to get her hands free to press against his chest, pushing, pushing.

Tears welling up in her eyes, streaming down her cheeks, and then suddenly a snapping sound, and her whole body goes quiet.

Trevor breathes for both of them, and moments later the pressure takes its leave of her and snakes down through her body and drips out from between her thighs.

They part ways on the landing. She never does get to Luscious, but chooses instead to head back home. Luscious has a keen eye and sharp nose. She'll know about Campbell as soon as she walks through the door.

She decides to take her chances with Millie instead. Millie's mind is always on Fred. She'll have a better chance with Millie.

On Christmas Day, just after Luscious called for a third helping of pie and Great-uncle Nate decided just to go head-on and set the bottle of Bourbon down between his legs instead of hoisting his heavy frame up off the couch each time he needed to refill his glass, the doorbell rang.

They weren't expecting any more people, but it was Christmas, and Millie didn't care if the whole world stopped in. She was happy that Fred had finally bought her those diamond earrings from JCPenney and Luscious hadn't picked on her too badly and the turkey had turned out perfect and so had the yams, so Millie was smiling when she answered the door.

There weren't any leaves left on the trees by the time December arrived, but there they were, floating in with the winter wind, like it was October or even the second week in November.

Millie's smile just vanished. It didn't fade, slip, or crumble; one second it was there, and the next it was gone.

"Yes?" Millie says, and she might as well have said, "What you want, bitch?" because that's how deadly it sounded.

"Fred here?" the woman says, and Campbell moves closer, because the leaves and the sound of Millie's voice have her all confused, and she sees a glimpse of that faux-fur wine-colored collar.

Fred pushes Campbell aside, and she looks into her father's face to try to understand what this is all about, but it's blank—and when his eyes lock with the woman's, he's so cool he don't even blink, and even the woman is taken aback, and she squints at Fred to make sure that this is the same man who'd held her in his arms just two days ago and assured her that he was leaving his wife and child to be with her.

"Fred," she says, and his name is like worn velvet on her tongue.

"Yes?" Fred says, and squints at her like he's never brushed her hair and stepped in behind her in the shower and kissed her in places on her body he hadn't even considered on Millie in months.

Millie is breathing so hard that Campbell can see the tops of her breasts pushing out from below the scooped neck of the red pullover she's wearing.

The little girl, with her sweet round eyes and smiley face, is looking at Fred the way Campbell looks at him, and her heart speeds up, and she starts taking breaths like Millie because she knows what's happening now; she understands completely.

"Did you tell her?" The woman leans on one big leg and tilts her head to the side like she's tired. Campbell knows if they all weren't there, all of them around the door, Fred would have stepped forward and rubbed the fatigue from the crook of her neck.

He doesn't say anything, and Millie's hands are busy pulling at her pants, her head swinging between Fred, the woman, and the child.

Fred just sighs and pulls out his pack of cigarettes from his pocket. He looks down at the child and kind of smiles, and once again Campbell feels that if they all weren't there to see, he would have leaned down and tweaked her tiny button nose.

He pops a Winston in his mouth and then strikes a match, careful to cup the flame with his hands, protecting it from wind and Millie's heavy breathing.

"Close the goddamn door!" Great-uncle Nate slurs from the living room, and the toilet flushes upstairs—and Campbell knows that Luscious will be down soon and Fred better get to talking quick, 'cause Luscious don't warn nobody; she just surveys the situation and commences to swinging.

"Fred, what this woman want?" Millie manages to say. Her words bounce off each other and then seem to echo.

Fred just puffs on his cigarette, and the smile he offered the little girl is looking kind of strained now, and his left eye has begun to tic.

"I said what this woman—"

"She belong to him. He ain't tell you?" The woman cuts Millie's words off and pushes the little girl an inch closer. "You ain't said nothing to them, Fred?"

All eyes fall on Fred.

Luscious, already down the stairs, takes a moment to digest what she's just heard before reaching past Campbell for Fred's throat.

There's a lot of commotion then. Fred struggling to get Luscious's fat fingers from around his neck, Campbell hollering, "Daddy! Daddy!"

The little girl hollers the same.

Millie's eyes roll between Luscious's back and the surprised face of the woman. She don't know who to hit first, but she wants to hit somebody, and so Campbell jumps up on the stairs and moves three steps up and out of the way.

Great-uncle Nate gets up, red-eyed, bottom lip fat and hanging, Bourbon bottle in hand, and zigzags across the room, swinging the bottle up and into the air, taking drunken aim at Fred and missing him by a mile, the bottle shattering on Luscious's shoulder.

"You asshole!" Luscious screams, still holding on to Fred's throat, while using her free hand to snatch the broken bottle out of Nate's hand.

"Luscious, let go of him. He ain't worth it," Millie says, real soft. Because the way Luscious's eyes looked, if mama screamed her words, all it would do was to add fuel to the furnace that was boiling inside of Luscious's body.

"You kill him, and they'll send you back," Millie adds.

Campbell hears those words and takes a step down. *Back where?* she wonders.

Luscious hears her sister's words, and her eyes seem to clear— and after a while she lets go of Fred, and he falls, coughing, to the floor.

"You're an animal, Rita! They needed to have kept you—"

Luscious takes a threatening step toward Fred, and his mouth clamps right up.

"You ain't nothing but a sorry piece of shit," she says, and then she spits right in his face.

Campbell looks to the open door to find that the woman and child are gone; all that's left are the swirling autumn leaves.

For days there is only the sound of the television, footsteps, and the drip-drip sound of the kitchen faucet Fred never seems to have time to fix.

Millie takes to bed, and Fred takes up residence on the couch.

Campbell survives on cold-cut sandwiches until one day Luscious calls and tells her to come over after school.

"They still ain't talking," Campbell says as she looks through the bag of precooked food Luscious has packed up for her.

"Yeah, well, that's better than them yelling, screaming, and beating each other up," Luscious says as she reaches into the freezer, allowing her hand to move over three packs of chicken and two boxes of chocolate ice cream before finally coming to rest on a box of cherry Popsicles.

"That woman been back?" Luscious asks as she pulls out two pops and hands one to Campbell.

"Nah."

"That's your father, but what he done is a bad thing. Very bad."

"You think that really Daddy's child?" Campbell asks, even though she knows it is. They have the same mouth and eyes.

"Yep," Luscious answers a little too quickly.

Campbell looks down to the floor and shuffles her feet in embarrassment for her father.

"Men ain't shit," Luscious says, and shakes her head in disgust.

"What Mama mean about you going back?" she says because she wants Luscious to feel the same shame she feels. "Going back where, Detroit?"

Luscious blinks like something smarts or like she's got a gas bubble in her chest. "What you wanna know?" she says, and pulls the chair out from the table.

Campbell's tongue clucks, and the words get caught behind her teeth. She expected resistance. "W-What mama was talking about," she says, trying to keep the surprise out of her voice.

Luscious looks down at her ice pop and then back to Campbell, and when she does the green of her eyes is black and Campbell's not sure anymore if what Luscious has to say is anything that she wants to know.

Luscious smiles a bit, a crooked sneer, really. *It would be wise,* she thinks, *to tell Campbell everything. Tell her about the evil men do to young girls and women.*

Luscious bites off the head of her ice pop and leans back into her chair. *It would be good*, she thinks again, and her head bounces in agreement.

Before she was Luscious, she was Rita.

Little wide-eyed Rita, daughter of Erasmus and Bertha Smith, hardworking peoples who knew God, but not every Sunday.

They drank some and sometimes too much. Played their Billie Holiday records for the neighborhood, whether their neighbors wanted to hear them or not. Loved more than they fought, but fought just the same, had the scars and broken knickknacks to prove the latter, Rita to prove the first.

Before she was Luscious with a number and a cell mate, she was Rita of Detroit. Rita of Cadillac Avenue. Tall, redboned Rita, who swayed down the street on long lovely legs so well oiled, they gleamed. Rita with the green eyes and good hair that touched the middle of her back. Rita so fine, the white people forgot her thick lips and broad nose.

Before she was Luscious of Brooklyn, Luscious of Stanley Avenue, she was just Rita, minding her own business, who one day looked up into the eyes of her father's best friend and saw something there that she'd seen only in the eyes of schoolboys and lately strange men who beckoned her and sometimes brushed their fingers against her arm when she ignored their calls.

Manny Evans, raven-colored, bald-headed, broad-smiling, pockets-heavy-with-nickels Manny.

Manny Evans, who had bounced Rita on his knee, had patted the top of her head, dropped nickels into her savings jar, the old mayonnaise jar Bertha had cleaned and put aside for just that purpose.

Manny Evans, who had women on corners and a .22 in his

sock. He wore taps on the heels of his shoes, and the *nickel-jingle-clickety-click* sounds he made when he walked down the streets told everybody he was coming, but no one messed with him because they were sure about the .22 in his sock but suspicious about the breast pocket of his jacket or the nickel-free pocket of his pants.

Rita had always liked the way his head shone, but as she got older she began to appreciate his color, so black and smooth. She found herself thinking about his shoulders and the gold pinky ring he wore, the one with the black onyx stone. "Black like me," he said, "strong like me."

Rita filling out in places, eyes greener now, hair loose instead of pulled back, stockings replacing kneesocks, ears pierced, and Rita all the time licking her lips, keeping them moist, keeping them shiny.

Manny Evans dropping paper money in her savings jar instead of nickels, wanting to pat her ass instead of the top of her head, wanting to bounce her on his knee again and maybe on something else.

He visits on Saturday nights. Comes by with a bottle of whiskey after checking on his women, collecting money, and laying his hands on people who've allowed their eyes to slide over and past him when he called out to them, "You got my money, Niggah?" Erasmus and Manny drink, smoke Pall Malls, and play dominoes while Bertha talks to Adele from next door. Adele, tall like a man, with hands that wrinkled early and callused two years ago on the palms.

Before she was Luscious on parole and scrubbing floors for white folk in Indian Village, she was Rita, and that's what was written on her bedroom door in big black letters so Manny couldn't have mistaken it for the bathroom. But he did.

His fly is down, and his dick is already in his hands when he stumbles in, stinking of liquor and bleary eyed. He apologizes when he walks in on her in the middle of drying her just-bathed body, but he don't jump back and close the door or drop his eyes in shame. He just stares at her, and his hand, the one not holding on to his dick, reaches behind him and pushes the door shut.

His eyes enjoy her face and then her naked breasts and finally the thin line of black hair that begins two inches below her navel.

Before she was Luscious, she was Rita, confused and held down in her own bed by strong hands. Those same hands covering her mouth, roughly touching and rubbing. Those hands are rough, like the steel wool Bertha scrubs the pots with, and Rita believes that her skin will shred beneath them. She can't imagine a more painful feeling, and then she doesn't have to because he's inside her, pushing into the place where only her index finger had ever been.

Rita, before she was Luscious, her mind bending and her body coming apart on the inside and Manny not allowing her to scream or breathe, and when he's done he don't even look at her—he just looks down at the bloodstains on his pants and tucks back in the paper money sticking out of his pockets, but he leaves the nickels that have fallen onto the bed.

Manny Evans finds the bathroom just fine now and returns to Erasmus, his Pall Malls, and liquor and proceeds to win three more domino games.

Rita buds in the spring along with the knurly limbs of elms and oaks. Her belly pushes out in mid-April, coinciding with the tulip and daffodil blooms, and all the beauty of the season rests in the glow of her skin, but her eyes are as cold as the long-gone winter.

"Who?" Her parents ask, even though their minds have wandered over the young men who have spent time with Rita on the porch, the ones who called out to her from open car windows, music blasting, Rita's name lost in the lyrics and strain. They assume Jake's son Marshall or the Tompkins boy, Pierce.

"Coca-Cola man," Rita says, rubbing her stomach and looking off at nothing. Erasmus can't stop smoking, and Bertha keeps moving her hands up and down her arms.

"The Coca-Cola man?" they say together, and exchange glances before looking back at Rita.

"Hmmm," Rita sounds, and looks down at her swollen bare feet. "Mama, where the pail at?" she asks as if the conversation is over.

Bertha remembers her own pregnancy and her feet, swelled up and burning at the bottoms, but she can't go for the pail because Erasmus is reaching for another cigarette—even though the one he lit a moment ago is still burning in the ashtray.

"White man, then?" Erasmus asks, and then holds his breath.

Rita's eyes roam around the kitchen and then look up at her father. "No. Colored man," she says, and her eyes move to the ceiling and then down to the floor and then to the window that looks out into the yard.

"Girl, have you taken leave of your senses?" Erasmus laughs before lighting his cigarette and inhaling. His laughter is reeling, and it makes the hair on Bertha's neck stand.

"Why you say that, Erasmus?" Bertha asks, moving closer to Rita.

Erasmus's laughter rocks him, and his cigarette falls from his mouth.

"What's so funny? Why you laughing so?" Bertha's head swings between her husband and her child. "Man, you crazy or something?" she asks, rubbing at the hairs on her neck and taking another step that puts her right next to Rita.

Erasmus composes himself and bends down to retrieve his cigarette from the floor. Both women see the thin sheath of hair on the top of his head, and Rita thinks that in a few years he will be bald like Manny. She shivers.

"This here is 1942," Erasmus says, wiping the tears from the corners of his eyes and sticking the cigarette back between his lips. "And I ain't never seen no colored man driving no goddamn Coca-Cola truck!" Laughter consumes him again, and the house seems to shake with it.

It's too late to sit her in a tub of mustard water. Rita is too far gone for that, so they send her over to Fenton, over to Mamie Ray's place.

Mamie Ray, black, short and stout with a tangled mass of orange hair that spread out around her head like a feathered hat imparting her with a buffoon-type peculiarity. She had a dead right foot that was larger than her left and hands too small for her body, or even a five-year-old, for that matter.

When Rita stepped off the bus, Mamie Ray, body lopsided from years of dragging around her dead foot, was standing on the curb, waiting.

"You Rita?" Mamie asked as she grabbed Rita's elbow with her tiny hands. She hadn't really had to ask that question; Bertha had described her child to a tee, and all Mamie needed to look for were the eyes. "Ain't seen another pair like 'em, ever," Bertha had said to Mamie on the phone.

"Yessum," Rita said, her eyes struggling with the woman's orange hair and twisted body.

"How far along you think you is?" Mamie asked, looking down at Rita's stomach.

"Don't know," Rita replied, and took a step backwards.

"Well, you know when you 'llowed him on top of you. What month it was?"

"I ain't allow nothing," Rita mumbled. "Cold month, I suppose," she added, and chanced a glance at the oversized foot.

Mamie bit her lip and scratched at her head. "After Thanksgiving but before Christmas and New Year's?"

"I dunno," Rita said, and her eyes moved to the tiny hands.

"Uh-huh," Mamie sounded, and then, "You look strong; you can carry that suitcase." She wobbled away.

The women who came to see Mamie Ray came fruitful, bellies still flush, hips spreading, though, and breasts heavy and sensitive to the touch. They came dry mouthed, light-headed, always spitting puke, and always scared.

Rita thought most of them were ignorant, not ignorant about how it had happened, but *how it had happened to them.*

Some came wearing the cheap pieces of jewelry their lovers had given them, tacky tokens of affection that bent and turned colors, the mock gold fading and flaking away over time. Just like the men, just like their love.

Rita was too far gone for an abortion; she would stay through delivery and then return home, no one the wiser.

The other women, the ones who wore shame on their faces like masks, they would be gone, if things went well, within twenty-four hours.

Millie Blythe arrived just as June slipped into its last day. She was much younger than Rita, pale skinned with thin reddish-brown hair and large empty eyes. Feeble looking and thin, and Mamie took one look at her and was about to turn her away when her mother shoved roughly through the doorway and into the house.

"She look sickly," Mamie said after taking another look at Millie.

51

"She fine. Always look that way," the mother said, and then hastily slapped Millie's hands away from her mouth. "I done told you 'bout that," she snarled.

Mamie looked at the mother and then down at Millie's fingers. The child had chewed her nails clear down to the cuticle. "How far along is she?" Mamie asked, her eyes moving to Millie's vacant ones.

"Just about a month."

"How old is she?" Mamie squinted at the girl. Millie's body didn't have a curve to it.

"She old enough," the mother spat, and then shot Millie a look of disgust.

"Fourteen?" Mamie asked, ignoring the woman's sarcasm.

"Eleven," the woman said, and then cast a cold eye on Mamie.

Mamie didn't stumble back in surprise, but the hand that held her cane did begin to shake. "Eleven? Lord," she whispered. She'd never had one that young. "She still a baby," Mamie said more to herself than to the woman.

"Look, you gonna do it or not?" The woman's tone was like steel.

"I—" Mamie started to decline again and took a step toward the door; her fingers brushed against the doorknob just as the woman moved toward her.

"I'll pay you double what you usually charge," she said, and shoved three crisp fifties in Mamie's face.

Mamie liked the horses, loved to watch them run. She knew some of the jockeys and had had the opportunity to move her hands across the strong backs of the horses, down their muscular limbs and through their shining manes.

In the stands, her body quivered at the sound of their hooves galloping against the soft dirt of the track, making her feel a way no man was ever able to do.

She was a week behind with Otis the protector, who came to collect once a month. He had connections with the police department, and she had to pay him to make sure they would leave her be.

The oil tank had been empty since Memorial Day, but she was careful to keep up with the electric bill, because she did most of her work at night. For now, meals would be cooked on the hot plate, and showers would be taken in cold water. She'd straighten the mess out with the oil company in the fall just before the first frost hit.

So the money that Millie's mother was dangling in her face could have been used wisely, but the sounds of hooves beating like a hundred hearts were already pounding away in Mamie's ears.

"Come and get her tomorrow 'round noon." Mamie said, snatching the money from the woman's fingers.

The heat that followed Millie's arrival was stifling and generous, filling up every inch of the house. So intense, the old paint bloomed and puckered in places on the walls, and the doorjambs swelled and buckled.

Even though there were three empty bedrooms in the house, Mamie Rae put Millie in the room with Rita.

"There," Mamie said, indicating the empty bed next to Rita's even though there was another on the other side of the room.

In order to better handle the heat, Rita had stripped herself down to her drawers. She stretched out across the bed on her back, her belly and breasts like mountains of flesh.

"That there is Rita," Mamie said, and walked out of the room.

Millie stood in the doorway, her eyes wide at the sight of Rita.

"You ain't never seen no naked woman before?" Rita asked as she lifted each heavy breast and wiped at the perspiration that had formed beneath it.

Millie's hand shot up to her mouth, and her eyes dropped to

the floor as she moved to sit down on the bed. Rita's eyes moved with her.

Rita watched Millie's head bob and her neck twist and listened to the soft chewing sounds her mouth made as she devoured her cuticles.

When she couldn't take any more, she rolled onto her side and eased herself up on her elbow and said, "Ain't you been fed?"

Millie took a moment to answer. She slowly raised her eyes, and they immediately settled on Rita's heavy breasts, so she dropped them again. "Yes, ma'am," she whispered.

"Ha!" Rita laughed, "I ain't nobody's ma'am, girl!"

Millie said nothing.

Rita cocked her head and asked, "How old you is?"

"Eleven," Millie squeaked, and her eyes came up again.

"Eleven?" Rita eased her free hand down between her legs and scratched.

"Uh-huh."

"What's your name?"

"Millie," Millie said, coughed and then, "Blythe."

The child was soaked through with sweat by then. The fine red hairs curled against her forehead and dangled around her ears.

She wiped at her face and then the back of her neck.

"Go on and take off your clothes. Ain't nothing but females in this house," Rita breathed, and then looked off to another part of the room in order to give Millie some privacy.

Millie looked around the room and then hesitantly started to unbutton the delicate white blouse she wore.

Rita waited until the blouse was off and then the gray pleated skirt. When Rita turned to look at her again, what she saw was a pale thin line of a child with knocked knees and swollen ankles.

"You pregnant?" Rita was perplexed.

Millie's eyes rolled around in her head and then moved to the tattered window shutters. "Swallowed a watermelon seed."

"What?" Rita laughed.

"Watermelon seed. Swallowed one."

"Why you here, then?"

"Mama say Mamie gonna take it out so's that it won't grow inside of me."

Rita bit her bottom lip. "You get your monthly?"

Millie looked down at her hands. "Come January till May, and then I swallowed the watermelon seed and it stopped."

Rita eased herself up and swung her legs over the side of the bed. "Who gave you the watermelon?"

"Clyde."

"Who's that?"

"My mama's boyfriend."

"Uh-huh. Sliced it up for you, took it out of the rind and all?"

"Yeah. Most times."

"Other times?"

"We played a game."

"I play games, too. What kinda game? Maybe I knows it."

"He pops the watermelon in his mouth and then pass it to me."

"Pass it how?"

"He press his lips to mine, and push it into my mouth."

"I don't know that game."

"We play it all the time."

"That's how you got the watermelon seed?"

"Uh-huh."

Millie scratched at her nose and then rubbed her eyes before falling back onto the bed.

"He ever put the watermelon seed any place else?"

Millie said nothing.

"Y'all play other types of games?"

"Mama said I wasn't to talk about those."

Millie laid herself down and soon after was fast asleep, her loud snores filling the hot room.

Mamie came for Millie in the evening, just past eight, when the streets outside began teeming with people. There was a jazz club two blocks down, a bar across the street, and a chicken and rib shop next door. A Friday night in July on Pearl Street could seem like Saturday midday any place else in the country.

"C'mon, girl," Mamie Ray called out, and walked away.

Millie stirred from her sleep. "Okay. Coming," she yelled back as she reached for skirt and blouse.

"You ain't gonna take no bath, you know," Rita said, suddenly mad. Mad at Clyde, Millie's mother, and Mamie Ray.

"What?"

"You answering like Mamie just ran your bath water."

Millie just looked confused.

"It's serious what's Mamie's about to do to you," Rita whispered.

Millie cocked her head. "Mama said it wouldn't hurt a bit," Millie said, her bottom lip beginning to tremble.

Rita was already sorry.

"I—I . . . Don't mind me," Rita said, waving her hands at Millie. "The heat makes me mean." She offered her a grin.

Millie leaned forward and looked real hard at Rita's face.

"Go on, a little ol' watermelon seed ain't gonna hurt none." Rita's grin wavered behind her lie. There was an awkward moment, and then Rita stepped forward and embraced Millie.

"C'mon, girl!" Mamie Ray screamed from down the hall.

When Millie came back to the room, escorted by Mamie Ray, she was ashen, almost bleached-looking and seemed smaller, thinner. Her mouth hung open on one side, and her eyes, glassy and moist, rolled about in their sockets.

Rita averted her attention to the floor and then the window. As nice as Mamie Ray had been to her, she hated her at the moment.

Always hated her after the abortions. Hated the smell of ether and the screams that followed. Hated her even more the next day after the sheets (soiled yellow in places where the blood had been scrubbed away) were hung out to dry.

Mamie Ray laid Millie down onto the bed, and without a word turned and left the room.

Rita had heard Millie's screams, heard the child howl out in pain, the pleas for God and Mama and then the pitiful, confused, Why, why, why!

Millie had lost the very last bit of her childhood, the small piece that her mama's boyfriend hadn't been able to kill, the part of her that still looked forward to ice cream, doll babies, and Christmas.

Now Millie lay there, whimpering, clutching her stomach, and whispering for her mother.

Rita stayed put, right in her bed, her eyes holding on to the people who moved up and down the sidewalk outside the window, her mind trying to catch hold of the music that slipped from behind the door of the bar whenever someone came or went. She could separate herself from the sounds of Millie's body moving against the starched white sheets; she could dislodge herself from the moans and pretend the sick smell that was rising off Millie's feverish body was barbecued ribs.

An hour passed, and Rita's eyelids began to droop; her mind was out on the sidewalk keeping pace with the high-stepping colored folk. Rita's head had even begun to bob, and a slight smile puddled at the corners of her mouth because her baby was still again, allowing Rita to escape from the cube-size room and Millie's suffering.

Her hand was on the doorknob to the bar; she was easing the door open, pulling it back, and letting the music creep over her, her foot dangled over the threshold as she peered into the smoke-filled room. Rita could hear laughter, laughter that seemed to soar, reaching a pitch that took over the music and caused the smile to leak away from Rita's lips.

When Rita was thrown back to the room, her eyes flew open and found Millie, white and lifeless in a puddle of blood.

Millie's mama didn't seem too sad. Her eyes were wet, but Rita thought that might have been from the smoke coming off the cigarette she never stopped puffing on.

A man came with her. Rita supposed he was the one, Clyde, the watermelon seed passer. He was short and well built, like the football players who practiced out in the field behind Rita's house.

Rita had stared at him good and hard the whole time he was there—looking sad and holding Millie's mama's hand—and still she couldn't see the defect, the sick twisted part of him that would make him touch a little girl that way.

She'd half expected to see tiny horns pushing out from his scalp or a tail bulging from the back of his pants. Her eyes dropped to his shoes—could she detect a hoofed foot?

She was disappointed to find that his eyes were brown and warm, not the tiny, yellow, beady things she'd expected to see.

His hands moved to Millie's mother's shoulders; Rita saw that his pinky was absent the gold ring weighed heavy with onyx that was a sure sign of perversion and distrust.

The man reached into his pocket and pulled a ball-shaped peppermint from its depths. The crackle of the paper upset the mournful silence of the room, and Mamie Rae pulled the sheet over Millie's head just as he popped the candy in his mouth.

There was nothing, nothing at all that Rita could see in him that could warn her he was evil, and so she would walk wary through her years and never allow her trust to settle on any man. Ever.

Bertha has already been preparing, eating late and heavy. Drowning her biscuits in butter and then dabbing them in honey. She bakes pies and cakes and consumes them like air. She excuses herself from the conversations that take place around the bus stop in the mornings and evenings, when she's traveling to and from work. She excuses herself to spit or to move herself beneath the shade of a nearby tree and dab at the imaginary sweat forming on her brow and below her nose.

She calls in sick, falls out in front of the church after service is over and the congregation and choir are gathered out front.

She does all this so they can assume before she has to tell them.

Her hips have already spread, and people remember that she carried Rita the same way. "That baby is all in your behind, girl!" they say, just as she had planned.

"When you due?"

The questions come like rain.

"Lawd, you want another one after Rita practically grown!"

"My friend Ann had a baby late, too. Change-of-life baby— you probably won't even get your menstrual after this one come."

Erasmus didn't like what Bertha was doing, didn't like it one little bit. "Bertha, why we gotta hide the fact that Rita done gone and got herself knocked up?"

" 'Cause."

" 'Cause what?"

"Just 'cause." Bertha was done talking about it and went to check on the corn bread, chicken, and dumplings she was cooking.

She's been preparing, so that when Rita's labor pains started two days before the Independence Day celebrations—hitting her down between her legs and then exploding in her belly like the firecrackers that went off outside her bedroom window—Bertha was already good and fat and looking every bit like she was ready to drop.

Rita before she was Luscious, not called upon to change a diaper or heat a bottle, was assured that she would never be referred to as Mama or have to attend a PTA meeting. Bertha is Mama, and Rita before she was Luscious is just older sister, eldest sibling, first child of Erasmus and Bertha, mother of none.

"What you think we should call her?" Bertha asks when she hold the child in her arms.

Rita thinks about Millie, about the life she had and thinks maybe some good can come out of this whole thing and decides maybe she can give Millie a second chance at something better.

"Millie." She says, "Let's call her Millie."

They notice her breasts before anything else. Their eyes light on them like flies on sugar, and they lick their tobacco-black lips and drag their hands through their woolen hair, and some touch themselves, running their fingers across their chins or pinching the skin of their necks.

The women turn cold eyes on her, and one even spits in her path; another fixes her mouth to sling an insult but catches the cold glint in her eyes—and the sun fastens onto something long, sharp, and silver sticking out from her coat pocket—and she thinks better of her comment and bites her tongue and turns her head away instead.

It's just before dusk, and the sun is looming and orange in the sky, people are huddled in bunches on the corners, and someone is already cussing up a storm in one of the apartments overhead.

Music is streaming out of Lou's Place, and Jake's Spot has set the first batch of porgies in the pan to fry.

Friday night in the Black Bottom, Paradise Valley.

Rita reaches the corner and turns left on Hastings Street. Broken glass litters the sidewalk, and there are bloodstains close by, and farther away a chalk outline of where the body fell dead.

That was last night, and not one person is talking about it because someone else was shot dead outside of Sonnie Wilson's place and another stabbed behind The Flame.

Too many dead people to talk about; living people got other things to worry about, and move up and down the walkways and don't even seem to notice the silhouette on the ground. They trample across its hands, legs, and face while they talk about fifths, fucking, no-good men, and badass kids.

Rita turns into the O Bar.

The door sits open, and the orange sun can't even work its way past the threshold; it's already midnight inside those walls, just the flicker of cigarettes and the dim light coming off the jukebox exist there.

Rita peers in before stepping inside and into the gloom. The two men who are seated at the bar turn their heads to consider her and decide after a moment that the drinks sitting in front of them are more interesting, and they dismiss her and turn back to their Bourbon-filled glasses.

A woman, satin colored, long and leggy, moves from the shadows and positions herself near the jukebox. Rita sees that the skin around her eyes is puffy and the lipstick she wears is the color of the purple-black grapes she gobbles down during winter. The woman drapes herself around the jukebox and presses the side of her face against the curved metal. Slowly, gently, she places loving kisses onto the glass, leaving plum-colored lips smeared across its clear face.

Rita watches her for a while before moving to the bar and taking a seat.

"Yeah," the bartender calls from a dark space at the end of the bar.

Rita squints her eyes. "Manny here?" she asks.

"Maybe," the voice calls back.

The two men turn their attention to Rita once more.

"He here or not?"

"Depending on who's asking."

"Tell 'im Rita here."

"Rita who?"

"Erasmus girl."

There is the sound of wood scraping against wood, and Rita catches sight of a worn white T-shirt and muscular brown arms as the bartender moves from his chair to a room behind the bar.

The woman is done with loving the jukebox and pulls up a stool next to Rita. The men exchange glances and then drop their eyes back down to their drinks.

"What you want Manny for?" The voice is coarse and brittle, and Rita's eyes turn on the puffed skin and scraggly gray strands sticking out from the black-blond hair.

"I got something for him," she says.

"Yeah, what you got that no other woman in here got? We all got something for Manny," the woman says, and a bitter laugh escapes her. "Gimme a smoke, Lester," she orders without allowing her eyes to let go of Rita's.

Lester almost tips his drink over as he hurriedly tosses a cigarette down the bar and then drops a dollar down next to his glass and rushes out the door.

The woman reaches into her bosom and pulls out a lighter. Her eyes still holding Rita, she lights the cigarette and inhales deeply. "They ain't nobody too young for Manny," she mumbles to herself, and then blows a stream of smoke into Rita's face. "Shit, I was young once, too, ya know," she spits, and slams her hand down on the counter. "Must be them eyes. You got eyes like a cat. Probably sneaky like 'em, too."

The man who was left sitting at the bar dug deep into his

pocket, pulled out a dollar, and dropped it next to his glass. "Later, Lonnie," he yells out over his shoulder before shooting Rita a cautious look and skip-walking out of the bar.

"Hey, Lonnie, he here or not?" Rita asks.

"He said he don't know no Rita or Erasmus," Lonnie says as he lazily flips through the newspaper.

"He don't know nobody he owe, had, or hates!" the woman laughs. "Ain't that right, Lonnie!" she screams, and slaps the bar again.

"If you say so, Ursula."

"So which category you fall under, honey?" Ursula leans in and whispers to Rita's cheek.

The rancid stench of Scotch and cigarettes accosts Rita's nostrils, and she stands up suddenly, sending the stool toppling down to the floor.

"Oooh! This one's a little spitfire," Ursula says. "Yeah, he like 'em like that."

"That's enough, Ursula," Lonnie warns, and finally moves from the dark end of the bar. He's large, over three hundred pounds, and his stomach jiggles beneath his T-shirt with every step he takes toward Rita.

"He ain't here. So either buy a drink or vacate the premises," he says, and lays his meaty hands down on the bar.

"He ain't here?" Rita questions sarcastically.

"He always here," Ursula whispers, and then breaks down with laughter.

Lonnie shoots her another warning look before turning his gaze back to Rita. "That's what I said." His tone is angry now.

Rita chews on her bottom lip for a moment. "Okay," she says, and then, "Where's the ladies' room?"

"For customers only!" Ursula screams, and pounds a scrawny fist on the bar.

Lonnie rolls his eyes and says, "At the back and to the left." He turns on Ursula. "I'ma throw your ass out of here, ya hear me, Ursula!"

Rita moves slowly toward the dewy blackness of the back. Cigarette smoke hangs heavy in the air, and the soles of her shoes makes sucking sounds against the sticky filth of the floor.

She walks slowly and turns her head slightly to see Manny seated in a large leather chair. He's leaning back, legs stretched out before him, arms folded across his stomach, onyx stone gleaming.

Lonnie is still fussing at Ursula, his sausage-length index finger swaying ominously in her face.

Rita moves right and slips behind the bar and into the room.

She stands there for some time, staring at his gleaming bald head, thick neck, and the hands that held her down. Her eyes roll over the legs that forced hers apart and shoes that left black polish streaks across her bedspread.

He sneezes, and his eyelids fly open; his brown eyes hold the green of hers, the young face soft, plump, and glowing of motherhood. He smiles a sleepy smile, and his eyes drop to her firm, full breasts and the small circles of wetness seeping through the pale pink blouse she wears.

Rita steps closer to him, and he smells the talcum powder she's dusted her stomach with, the sour milk the baby spewed across her skirt that Bertha dragged a wet cloth across before Rita walked out the door.

"What you doing here?" he finally asks when his eyes grow tired of holding her and the wet spots begin to make him uncomfortable.

Rita was still seeing the shoe polish marks on the bedspread and feeling the gold band of his ring pressed between her fingers, and she could hear her insides screaming, screaming and pulling apart and him breathing heavy in her neck, her hair, his skin slapping against hers and the tearing part complete and the silence that swelled inside of her and him so deep within her she feels as if her body will swallow him whole.

"What you want?" he asks, his voice filling with annoyance, his eyes looking behind her for Lonnie.

Rita wonders why she's so calm, so cool, and she looks down at her hands that aren't even shaking and thinks about her heart that barely beats enough for her to breathe right anymore and looks at Manny and relives every horrible minute of that night and Millie's death and the Watermelon Man and her daughter's birth, and there's nothing but pain, suffering, and sorrow attached to all those memories, and Manny is the source of it all, and so she reaches into her pocket and pulls out the knife that Bertha uses to gut fish, and before Manny can understand what's happening, before he can move his big hands to stop her, she brings the knife down and into his heart.

A screaming Ursula backs away from the doorway, her purple lips a large circle, her chicken-thin hands cradling her cheeks as Rita, bloody hands and blouse soaked through with mother's milk, moves past her.

Somewhere on Belle Isle Bridge, black and white boys pound away at each other, and days later when the police knock on Bertha's door to come and take Rita away, the O Bar is burned down to the ground when white rioters tossed firebombs through the glass panes of businesses along Hastings, Saint Antoine, and Brush.

By the time Rita is assigned her number and asked to turn front and then sideways for the camera, Manny Evans's chalky silhouette has burned away to nothing, and Rita is on her way to becoming Luscious #132541289.

Luscious lays a heavy hand on Campbell's shoulders; she wants to tell Campbell that she is her *granddaughter-niece* and that

Millie is her *daughter-sister*, but that secret has been with her for so long that she hardly knows what's true and what's not, so she swallows hard on that reality and looks deep into Campbell's eyes, and Luscious says, "Someone hurt me once, and I hurt them back—and for that, I was sent away."

"Jail?" Campbell whispers as her eyes go wide.

"Yes," Luscious breathes. Her mouth goes bitter with the memory of it, and she sucks off the last piece of cherry ice from the Popsicle stick. Campbell looks at Luscious's red, wet lips, and she thinks about blood and shudders.

"See you next week, then?" Luscious says as she reaches for the freezer door again.

Campbell nods her head and eases quietly out the door.

Millie said that she would make her marriage work even if it killed her. Well Fred's bastard had almost done just that.

The thought of her, those eyes so much like her Fred's, her color, exactly the same, looking everything like Campbell did when she was that age—it was poison.

But yet Fred remained. Walking, sleeping, and eating in that house as if he'd done nothing wrong. Nothing at all.

Luscious called Millie a fool. "Put his ass out!" she'd screamed.

Finally, she did. Packed Fred's stuff up, set it out on the stoop, and had the locks changed.

Campbell was waiting at the window when Fred walked down the block, five hours after he had gotten off work.

What stunned her most wasn't the three minutes he stood outside the gate, staring at the boxes and the glint of new metal on the door. What stunned her most was the smile that covered his face. She'd never seen her father smile that broadly.

She half expected him to jump up and click his heels together when he jumped in front of the gypsy cab that was barreling down the street.

The boxes, just four of them, were loaded into the trunk and wide backseat, and Fred didn't even give his house one last look before he climbed into the front seat beside the driver and sped happily away.

Later that night after Millie takes two of her special aspirins and downs three cans of beer, Campbell turns to her journal and writes.

Men leave. Even daddies.

Millie notices that January has come and gone and the box of sanitary napkins she's bought for Campbell still lay waiting at the bottom of her closet.

She misses the five days out of the month Campbell usually hand-washes her panties and hangs them to dry over the shower rod. The Tylenol she asks for on the first day when the cramps are unbearable.

These things would have escaped her a few months ago, when Fred was still there. But Campbell is all she has now, and she concentrates on her daughter to keep from thinking about the absence of her husband.

Those things, along with the dreams she has about fish and Fred and babies hanging from trees, falling from the sky like rainwater and popping up in pumpkin patches, make her look at Campbell one day, really look at her, and when she does she sees clearly the extra seven pounds and the glow in her daughter's cheeks.

But she isn't angry. Not at Campbell. She is angry with herself and the years she's spent running behind a man she'd trapped into marrying her to begin with. Wouldn't have been so bad, though, wouldn't have been so bad if she'd loved him to begin with. She'd needed him first; the love came later.

What type of mother was she?

Unfit and wrong, she supposed. Stupid and foolish and lacking the motherly sense it took to keep proper watch over her one and only child.

Her feet take the last step, and her hands grip the banister.

Who was she to think that her life could unfold like some goddamn television show? A thirty-minute *Leave it to Beaver* episode that always ended on a high note and never with illegitimate children, court appearances, and pregnant teenagers.

She steadies herself in front of Campbell's bedroom door.

Millie would take the blame for this one, and wouldn't even go word for word with Fred about the whole thing, and when Luscious pointed the finger of blame, Millie would take her place right in front of it.

Months later, Campbell would find herself standing in front of Trevor Barzey's door again, belly straining against the waistband of her jeans, breasts heavy and uncomfortable in one of Millie's bras, Fred on her left and Millie to her right, Luscious fuming somewhere in the background, strangers looking out at them from the open doorway, and Campbell not able to meet their eyes when she whispers Trevor's name.

"Oh, the people who lived here before?" the strangers advise in broken French, "They moved, long time ago."

Him

1971–1985

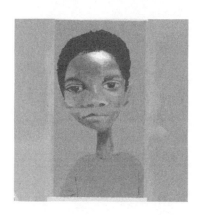

Age Seven

Donovan is the eldest of two; a girl just four years old and still in diapers walks so closely behind him he can smell the sour scent of her diaper.

He is seven, tall, and already cynical about the world.

"Stop following me," he whispers over his shoulder at his sibling, whose feet stop moving just as the words tumble from his mouth. He cocks his head and listens to the voices that slip from behind the half-open door to his parents' bedroom. He can't quite hear everything that is being said, so he creeps closer and so does baby Elaine.

Donovan shakes his head in dismay and shoves his hand behind him, catching his sister off guard and sending her tumbling backwards and then down to the floor.

There's a sick squishy sound as the diaper explodes and liquid squirts across the hardwood floors. Elaine opens her already big eyes in surprise and then giggles before pulling herself upright again and tottering toward him.

Donovan shakes his head in disgust and takes three more steps closer to the door. His parents, Solomon and Daisy, are arguing again. Solomon is getting on Daisy about her Saturday nights at the bingo hall, the bright pink lipstick she wears that reminds Donovan of the cotton candy he begs for on Sundays when they behave like a family and drive out to Coney Island.

Solomon is yelling about the denim shorts that stop right above her knees. He's pointing at the large hoop earrings; he says they make her look like Foxy Brown. "I thought you liked Foxy Brown!" Daisy screams back at him.

He's fussing about the auburn color of her hair ("It was black when I married you!"), the crimson-colored polish, dark lipsticks, and the white pants she likes to wear on the weekends when the weather is warm, the ones that draw men's eyes to her hips and hefty behind.

"White pants," Solomon screams, "should only be worn by whores and women without children or a husband!"

"Are you calling me a whore, Solomon?"

"If the shoe fits—"

"Drop dead!" Daisy screams, and Solomon rushes to hush her. He doesn't like scenes, hates for the children to hear them arguing and worse even, the neighbors. Solomon casts a hesitant glance toward the doorway and then as an afterthought kicks the door shut.

"I'm leaving you, Solomon—I can't take it anymore!"

Daisy is crying now, and Donovan can hear the dresser drawers opening and closing and the metal hangers clanging together as she rips her clothes from the closet.

"N-No Daisy, p-p-p-p-please."

"Uh-huh, Solomon, I've had enough."

"Daisy, I just want you to stay home and behave like a wife and m-m-m-mother."

Donovan hears his father stuttering, shaky voice, and he rolls his eyes.

"I—I—I l-love you, Daisy."

"Listen to him, blubbering, blubbering and stuttering like a goddamn baby." Donovan speaks to the door. His hands are on his hips, pinching the skin there, pinching it hard so he could have an excuse for the tears that are welling up in his eyes. Elaine has moved in beside him, careful not to touch him, trying her best to imitate his stance.

"If she wants to go, I say let her go. She's always wining about leaving, so leave already. We don't need her. I know I don't."

Donovan bobs his head a few times and folds his arms across his chest.

"Just go so we could finally have some peace and some god-damn quiet around here," he whispers, and quickly wipes away the tears that are moving down his cheeks.

Elaine folds her arms and bobs her head, too.

"You love me? Then why can't you trust me, Solomon? You follow me to the store; you follow me to work. You show up at the bingo hall—"

"I—I come to m-m-m-meet you because it's late."

"When did you become this—this—thing?"

"D-Daisy—"

"You know what the worst of it is, Solomon? Half of what you do is not even you—it's your mother!"

"N-No I—"

"You know what, Solomon. You're worse than a mama's boy—"

"D-Daisy, please!"

"—you're a Grammy's boy, and that's so much more despicable!"

"N-No, p-p-please—"

"You listen in on my phone calls, open my mail, call my girl-friends up, and ask them if we went where I said we where going. I've had enough."

"I—I'm s-s-s-s-s-sorry."

"Yes, you are, Solomon."

The door flies open, and Daisy almost walks over Donovan and Elaine.

"Go to your room," Solomon flings over his shoulder as he hurries behind his wife.

Donovan does not obey; instead he follows his parents down the hall and to the living room where the pink suitcase still sits, packed from the last time she threatened to leave. That was yesterday.

Donovan looks down at his sister. "I hope she takes you with her. You'll just grow up, make trouble, and leave, too," he says before he snatches Elaine's little hand and drags her off to their bedroom.

"D-Daisy, be r-r-rrrrrreasonable," Solomon says, and grabs Daisy by her elbow.

"Off!" Daisy screams, and jerks away from his grasp.

There is no departing door slam or indecent last word, not even good-bye, just the sound of her blue open-toed clogs clunking away down the hallway.

After Daisy left, she came back, stayed a year, and then packed Elaine up and moved out for good.

It was summertime, and Donovan would always remember that day: the fire hydrants open and spraying, flooding the streets, black children dancing, skipping, and screaming their way through the water, the trees heavy with green leaves and the sky a calm teal, the sun a large yellow moon at the center of all of that jubilance and him, sitting beside his father in that white two-door old Cadillac with the bucket seats and sunroof, the one Daisy had seen and wanted and got, just because she asked.

The one Solomon had had her name inscribed across the hood, her name with a long-stemmed rose that began at D and ended at Y. Her name that he had taken a steel wool pad to after she'd packed up and left for good, but who knows what the man had used for the rose, because the wool didn't even bruise it.

Donovan wanted to tell his father to turn the air-conditioning on; the seats were covered in plastic, and Donovan's T-shirt was soaked through with sweat, and his arms and bare legs were baked red by the sun.

Solomon didn't seem to notice the heat or the sun as he sped along with one arm hanging out the window, his fingers thumping the side of the car, right hand lightly gripping the steering wheel, his eyes wet as Al Green crooned "Let's Stay Together," from the eight-track player.

Donovan folded his arms across his chest and turned his head away in disgust.

They would have to move in with Solomon's mother, Solomon confided in him.

"It's best. Now that your mother is gone, you need some type of female handling," Solomon had said.

Donovan had just stared blankly at him. All his friends were here, his school was just two blocks away, and he didn't need no damn female handling—he was practically a man!

"Oh," Donovan said.

There wasn't much to take, just a few bags of clothes, a clock Solomon had wanted to keep, their wedding pictures, Daisy had said she couldn't care less about those. She would need all the furniture, though.

"All of it, Solomon. You're moving back in with your

mother—she don't have room for it. I'm starting all over again, and there's Elaine to think about."

Solomon gave in. Solomon always gave in.

Edna Evans-Barrows had been lovingly referred to as Grammy since she was child because of her wise eyes and old soul. Grammy was a tall broad woman with a sweet smile and razor-sharp tongue.

She was born and raised in Michigan, had lived in downtown Detroit for most of her life until her stepbrother Manny was killed by some jealous woman and then the riots came and everything familiar to her was either dead or burned down to the ground.

She'd met her husband, Homer Barrows, there. She'd liked the gray green of his eyes and the way he pulled back his hand and kicked out his leg after tossing lucky sevens in the dice games he frequented behind the O Bar.

She was sixteen and Homer was twenty and not the least bit interested in marriage, but when Manny found out what they'd done in the back of his Pontiac, he hung Homer by one foot over the railing of Belle Isle Bridge and threatened to drop him if he didn't do the right thing by Edna.

Manny said Homer had spoiled his sister. He screamed it over and over again: "You have de-flowered my little Grammy!"

Homer had begged for his life, praying out loud and trying hard not piss all over himself. But there was a split second when he stopped and almost cracked a smile.

He twisted his head upward to look Manny Evans in the eye. He wanted to say, "Negro, please! Your sister has had more dick than a little bit!"

But he didn't. The look said it all, and Manny uncurled one long finger from around Homer's ankle and Homer commenced to begging for his life again.

He and Grammy were pronounced husband and wife.

By the time Manny was dead, Homer and Grammy had relocated to New York, had had three babies, and she was heavy with the fourth. He could have walked out on her then with the threat of Manny buried and decaying in a Detroit graveyard. He could have just strolled west instead of coming home from work, but Grammy had a lot of her brother's ways in her, and had awakened him on more than one occasion with a straight razor pressed against his throat or the .45 she kept hidden from him pushed up between his legs, and those deadly threats reminded him that home was where the heart was and had better damn well remain.

Solomon was just three months old when Homer's courage overwhelmed him and he stood, belched, adjusted his pants about his waist, and walked away from them forever.

He died two months later, dropped dead on top of the woman he'd left Grammy for. The coroner told Grammy he was smiling when they picked him up. Grammy hadn't even shed a tear. There were no funeral arrangements made, just Grammy and her children milling outside the crematorium as Homer's body was burned to cinders.

She took him (what was left of him) back home to Detroit, where she dropped him, urn and all, over the side of the Belle Isle Bridge.

Grammy's daughters, all six of them, knew the truth. They'd witnessed it. The brawling fights that left their father beaten and bruised. The late-night visits from the police, the lies Homer told about his injuries.

"Had a little too much to drink and fell down the stairs, officers." "Walked right into that door and screamed holy hell, sir."

Grammy just sitting there, looking as cool as ever, even offering the policemen cookies and coffee, pound cake and tea.

They knew the truth, and when Homer walked away from them, they didn't blame him one bit but would hate him forever for leaving them behind.

There were hard times after Homer left. Hard times for the girls, but not for Solomon.

Grammy raised him on lies and nursery rhymes, filling his head with memories that belonged to some other mother, some other dead man's wife, because the stories that Grammy shared about Homer had to have been taken straight from the *Reader's Digest* periodical she subscribed to. None of what she told him about their twenty years of marriage was true.

Grammy took on two jobs to keep the bills paid, food in the refrigerator, and Solomon content. While the girls pushed cardboard into the bottom of their worn-out shoes and used rags between their legs when Grammy said there was no money for Kotex, Solomon was the only one who had two pairs of shoes and a pair of galoshes. He got a new winter coat every year and a new spring jacket every other year. No, Grammy couldn't spare the Vaseline— Solomon had a skin condition that required that she never run out, so the girls would have to use bacon grease for their skin.

He was sickly as a child, suffering all year long with ear infections and an on-again off-again stuttering problem, anemic and weak in the eyes, wearing bifocals by the age of five.

Grammy had nursed him straight through until he was four years old.

"With all that mother's milk, you'd think he would have been as strong as an ox," someone had ventured.

She would have nursed him long after that for all anyone knew, but a family member visiting from Michigan had witnessed in horror Solomon traipsing over to his mother, hopping up into her lap, and shoving his hand down the neck of her blouse in search of her tit.

The relative had blinked wildly and swallowed her words along with the hot tea she was sipping until the tea was gone and all that was left were the words. She narrowed her eyes and rested a light hand on Grammy's knee, leaned in and remarked in a hushed tone, "Some people might see that as unnatural, Edna."

Solomon slept alongside his mother until he was eight years old. Spooning himself into her back at night, breathing in the talcum powder scent of her skin, and moaning whenever her body eased away from him.

When he was thirteen and his limbs began to lengthen, the baby fat dropping away from his cheeks and middle section, his voice straining and cracking beneath the weight of his approaching manhood, Grammy had walked in on him unannounced and caught him touching himself, a battered, dogeared *Cosmopolitan* magazine thrown on the bed below him.

Grammy stood in shock for a moment, unable to close her mouth or even lift her hands to cover her eyes.

Solomon let out a groan of embarrassment and quickly tried to stuff his stiff member back into his underwear.

The seconds she stood there staring, mouth agape and hands fluttering about her waist and then finally resting on her arms, felt like hours until finally, she turned and walked out of the room.

They never spoke on the matter, and Grammy never walked in on Solomon again.

Grammy had to be mother and father to Solomon, taking time off work to sit in the stands during Little League and later football. She lovingly rested ice packs on his knees when he went out for track and massaged his back when he strained his muscles from lifting the weights he'd begged her to buy him for Christmas.

When the girls started coming around, calling on the phone, leaving silly little love notes covered with hearts and kisses in her mailbox, Grammy just smiled.

She was sure it would be years before he left her, not like Homer and her daughters, in a hurry to get away from her.

Grammy was sure that Solomon would be with her for a long, long time—and maybe even forever.

Daisy Watkins. Brown-skinned, skirt-too-short, perfume-too-loud Daisy. Grammy didn't like her from the beginning. She didn't appreciate her gap-toothed smile and freckled skin. "She must have some white in her," Grammy said after their first meeting.

"Great-grandmother, I think," Solomon had said, and Grammy could have sworn he swooned when he said it.

Solomon always on the phone running up her phone bill and spending all his time up in Harlem. Harlem! Chasing behind that girl and spending his money on cards and flowers and movies.

"Niggers uptown ain't been civilized since the Harlem Renaissance ended," Grammy said.

Solomon just nodded his head and laughed.

"What you got on you, boy?" Grammy asked, catching him by the arm and sniffing at his neck.

"Cologne, Grammy—dang!" Solomon bellowed, and tried to pull away from her, and that's when she saw the hickey.

"What the hell is that?" she asked, gripping him tighter and pulling him closer to her.

"What?"

"Don't *what* me, boy," Grammy yelled, and then pushed her index finger into the side of his neck. "This here bite mark, that's what."

Solomon cringed. "Ahh, that ain't nothing," he said, and blushed.

Grammy stepped back and folded her hands across her chest. "Ain't she got no upbringing? No class?"

Solomon just dropped his eyes.

"A real woman, a woman with class, wouldn't do thing. What's she trying to do, mark you so everybody wi you hers?"

Solomon said nothing.

"Animals do that, not people," Grammy said, and with that stormed out of the room.

It scared Grammy, this woman having so much of a hold on her one and only son. The boy didn't even walk anymore; he just floated. And every other sentence that came out of his mouth included her name. "Today Daisy and I—" "Did you know that Daisy—?" "I think that Daisy thought the same thing—"

It just made her sick. "Don't your mind run on anything other than Daisy?" Grammy spat.

Not only was his mind running on Daisy, but his heart was wrapped all around her, too.

"Marry who?" Grammy had scoffed and then laughed when Solomon sat down at the kitchen table and nervously told her of his plans.

"She pregnant?" she asked, and gave the pork loin a nasty jab with the knife she was holding.

"No, ma'am." Solomon was blushing.

"Then what you need to marry her for? You're too young, and you sure enough can't support a family working part-time at the post office."

Solomon swallowed hard before lifting his head, pushing out his chest and raising his voice some. "Got notice today that I'm full-time, with a route and everything."

Grammy jabbed the meat again. "Really?"

"Yes," Solomon said, and his voice quaked. Grammy was handling the news all too calmly.

"And you sure she ain't pregnant?"

"No, ma'am. I mean—yes, ma'am, I'm sure."

"You been there, then?" Grammy said, and turned to face Solomon.

"What—? I mean, excuse me?" Solomon grimaced and then his face went flat. Was his mother asking him what he thought she was asking?

"There," she said again, and pointed the sharp tip of the blade at his crotch. "Down between her legs. Sex. You sleep with her yet?"

Solomon twisted in his chair, started to say something, but his mouth just clamped up tight.

"You gotta be the first and only one there you know, 'cause if you the second, third, or tenth, she always going to have something to compare you to. And when things ain't going right—and believe me, in marriage, things don't always go right—she gonna think about that one she had, the one that might still be willing to be with her."

All the emotions that were streaking across Solomon's face melded together in surprise and then just slid off.

Satisfied that she was gaining some headway with Solomon, making the boy think some about his decision, she smiled and turned back to the meat.

"Just so you know, it's best if you the first 'cause if you ain't, you already starting out on the wrong foot. Full-time work or no full-time work. A woman that's been touched by more than one man can be a heap of trouble, and I ain't even going to get into them nasty sex diseases. . . ."

Her words went through Solomon and settled in a place that had been warm for Daisy from the first day he laid eyes on her.

And even after she gave herself to him he knew by the easy way he slid into her, the comfortable cozy feeling of her pink insides, the way she pulled him deeper and how she knew just how to touch him and where, that she had had someone else. Well, so had he.

But now Grammy made him wonder how many.

He'd had at least ten women, but that was okay for a man. That's what men did—that's what was expected of them, wasn't it?

Now those thoughts, those questions Grammy had just raised were slowly turning that warm place cold.

"I ain't never had no other man 'sides your daddy. Not ever." Grammy went on and on, and by the time she was done, that warm place was a block of ice.

Solomon approached Daisy about it. Hitched his pants and stood his ground like the man he'd always wanted to be, the strong man Grammy said his father had been.

They discussed it, fought about it, and then fell into each other's arms and cried about it until Daisy assured him that there had been just one other man, a man she thought she loved, but knew now that it wasn't that at all, not love, not like what she was feeling for Solomon.

They married at the justice of the peace, and Solomon didn't even spend the entire first night with his new bride, because Grammy didn't allow him to stay out past 2 A.M. "Man or no man, you going to respect my house." And he did, so he came in at a quarter to two and slipped the gold band off his ring finger and tucked it into his pants pocket before checking on Grammy, who was propped up in her bed, waiting.

Two more nights passed, and Daisy was left alone in their brand-new studio apartment in Jamaica, Queens, her mother on the phone trying to quiet her daughter's tears, her father in the background calling Solomon a "boy and not a man. What kinda man can't tell his mother he done married? Sneaking around with his own damn wife—what kind of shit is that?"

Daisy putting up with his silliness. Loving her husband after work and well into the night because it would take him little more than an hour to get home by two so he had to leave before 1 A.M. and "Don't worry, I'm going to tell her tomorrow," spoken in her neck when they said good-bye at the door.

A whole week had passed before he was able to finally tell Grammy. She had slapped him across his face and then caught him by his throat before she even realized what she was doing. That little hussy had stolen her son right from beneath her nose, and she would hate her for the rest of their married life.

Some months later, Daisy cut her hair and began wearing it puffed out on her head like those suede-vest-sporting, miniskirt-adorned, bead-wearing hippies who smoked those reefer cigarettes and ended their conversations with, "Peace, my brother."

Well, that's what Grammy said. Told her that straight to her face after Solomon had convinced her to have them both over for Sunday dinner.

"Babies do something to women. You know your sister Jackie had a wild spirit. Nothing I could do, but that baby, that baby calmed her right down," Grammy had whispered in Solomon's ear before they left.

Daisy was perplexed. "We said we would wait a few years."

"Well, I don't want to wait," Solomon said, and banged his water glass down on the table. The dangling earrings and leather band bracelet she wore seemed to mock him.

"But—but, we were going to try to save up for a house. We talked about London and Paris. . . ."

Regular black people don't go them places. He could hear Grammy in his ears.

"I want a baby. Those other things will come," Solomon said.

Break her spirit, calm her down.

Daisy folded, and Solomon dropped her diaphragm in the garbage among the baby peas, spare rib bones, and white rice they'd had for dinner.

She let her hair grow long again, and her belly pulled away from her and reached out into the world, her breasts ballooned out before her, and her nose spread across her face and the gap seemed more noticeable when she smiled her thick-lipped smile. She was ugly, and Grammy told her so. "Must be a girl child 'cause she taking all your beauty from you," she said with a laugh and quick pat to Daisy's belly.

Grammy had never thought she was beautiful.

The baby came in July, the hottest summer on record, born on the fifth, just missing Independence Day, a fate that followed him the rest of his life.

A boy, seven pounds three ounces. Long and yellow with a clean head and pug nose. He kept his eyes closed for three days. Fists balled up and toes curled under like he was scared—not just scared but petrified of what life had in store for him.

"Should name him Homer after your daddy," Grammy suggested when she came to see him.

Daisy was on the hospital bed between them, baby boy resting in her arms, Grammy on the side closest to the door, Solomon to her right blocking the July sun coming in through the window.

Her head bounced between Grammy and Solomon, and her eyes dared him to agree.

"Nah, we got a name for him," Solomon said, and glowed when he looked down at his son. "We gonna give him a name that starts with Daisy and ends with me," he said, and reached down to stroke the baby's balled fist.

Grammy pursed her lips and rolled her eyes.

"Donovan," Solomon said, and grinned.

Grammy flipped it over in her head a few times. "How that begin with her and end with you?" she asked, feeling they were making fun of her sixth-grade education.

Daisy said nothing.

"Daisy starts with *D* and Solomon ends with *N*, so Donovan." Solomon said, and then a full smile spread across his face.

Grammy considered that for a moment. "Why can't it start with you and end with her? You planted the seed."

Daisy just shook her head. There was no pleasing this woman.

After the children—Donovan first and Elaine some years later—Daisy's body reached its full and womanly potential. Round hips and ample bosom, plump ass bouncing beneath those white pants Grammy talked about and hated so much that she made Solomon hate them, too.

Men calling out to her, even if Solomon was right by her side pushing his mind to slip back to the first time they slept together and how unashamed she had been of her naked body, the way she guided his lips to her nipples, how her hips knew just when to turn, push and pull back when he was inside her.

He thought of those things even as he walked the pavement of every borough he was assigned to. The images blinded him; he couldn't even see the numbers on the doors, the BEWARE OF DOG signs on the fences or the names on envelopes, his mind all the time running on how many before him and now how many men since.

They moved to a two-bedroom apartment in the same building, where Donovan and Elaine shared a room, and Daisy got a phone extension in the bedroom, good for Solomon—good for him to pick up and listen in on her phone conversations when she thinks he's sleeping.

Girl talk, hair and nails, people at work, clothing, movies. "Did you hear that new song?"

Nothing that suggests another man. Nothing. But then, maybe they were talking in code. Grammy said women talked in code.

She should know; she was a woman.

He's delivering mail in Brooklyn and sometimes Staten Island, but he needs to be in Queens, close by, so that on Saturdays when he's working and she's home with the kids, he can pop by and make sure that she's home with the kids.

Those kids don't break her spirit or even calm her down; she still plays the music loud and even got the kids dancing and spinning along with her and then there are the Saturday night bingo games with her girlfriends and sometimes dinner and a movie, too. Daisy goes whether he agrees to it or not, walks right out the door, leaving the kids *he* wanted to have in his care.

Solomon can't see how he's going to take her down a notch and stop her from wearing that hot-pink lipstick and having her hair corn-braided and beaded at the ends.

Grammy says, "Let me think."

Daisy hangs in there, even though there ain't no house and no plans for one, even though Paris and London have been replaced in her head with just leaving—packing up her kids and getting far and away from Solomon and Grammy and that whole Barrows tribe, especially those stupid-ass sister-in-laws of hers who breed children like cattle and never say anything against their mama or their husbands.

But she hangs in there, and the arguments get worse and worse, and she leaves and comes back, leaves and comes back.

"This was who I was when you married me. You loved me for me then—what happened between then and now?" Daisy says for the umpteenth time.

Solomon's not sure about anything anymore except that she's not the wife she's supposed to be, and he hears Grammy's words in his head and says, "I want another baby."

Because Grammy thinks that two children aren't enough. "A third one would calm her down for sure."

That's it for Daisy. She's gone.

So there they were, Solomon and Donovan pulling up in front of Grammy's house, number 43 Saint Felix Street, Brooklyn, New York.

Three-story brick house, potted plants on each one of the eight steps that led up to the front door that was wide open, exposing the pink-and-white-striped wallpaper and carpeted staircase that led up to the bedrooms and the vacant apartment above that.

String beans and ham hocks cooking on the stove and corn bread cooling on the table, Donovan could smell all of that and the talcum powder on Grammy's body when she rushed to the door and wrapped her arms around him.

She held on much too long. He felt just the way Solomon felt against her when he was that age.

God had given her a second chance and a double blessing, Grammy thought.

Praise the Lord.

Age Nine

Clyde Walker was a distant relative who'd followed Grammy and Homer down from Michigan back in the fifties. He'd never married, and Grammy always thought that was such a shame because he was a good-looking man, hardworking and kind.

He needed a place to stay.

The basement would do—he'd lived in basements for most of his time in New York. The basement would do.

Private entrance, insulated walls, and lime-green indoor-outdoor carpet on the floor. Boiler might be a problem, Grammy warned. It gets noisy in the wintertime, but he could be sure it kept the whole house toasty and warm.

"I'd only need it for six months. No more than that."

Grammy smiled. "We'd love to have you."

"Going out West," Clyde confided over the second piece of apple pie Grammy rested down before him. "I just need a place till my money come through, and then I'm out West."

"Los Angeles?" Donovan chirped.

"San Fran-cisco!" Clyde bellowed, and slapped his hand down on the table. "The land of milk and honey." He laughed and then winked at Solomon. "I sure do like the honey, ya know?" He laughed again.

Solomon knew. But he hadn't had any honey since Daisy left him.

"You always moving about. Here and there, no one place can hold you down, huh?" Grammy said, and sat down to devour her own slice of pie.

"No one place and no one woman," Clyde said, and then winked again at Solomon.

"So what money you waiting on?" Solomon asked, desperately wanting to move the subject away from women.

Grammy's eyebrows went up. "That ain't none of our business, Solomon."

"It's okay, Edna." Clyde said. "Fell down a manhole the year before. Wintertime you know, snow piled up knee high." Clyde wiped at his mouth and then scratched his chin. "Fell right through it, broke my hip, and fractured my foot. Was out of commission for a few months. The ladies weren't happy about that, not at all."

Another wink and then the laughter. Solomon cringed.

"It's the city's responsibility to keep up on things like that, so since they didn't, they got to pay for their mistake."

Solomon nodded his head.

"My lawyers say another six months and my case should be settled. West coast been calling me for quite a while, quite a while," Clyde said.

Six months turned to eight and then twelve.

He'd become quite comfortable at 43 Saint Felix Street,

spending most of his day chatting with Grammy in the living room, shoes off, stubby toes pushing into the soft pile carpet. His belly heavy with Grammy's good cooking, heavy and spilling over the waistband of his pants.

Clyde winking and laughing and sometimes his hand lingering a little too long on Grammy's knee when he was trying to make a point or needed her to listen real careful to what he was trying to say, and Grammy blushing like some schoolgirl and sometimes resting her hand on top of his and looking a little too deeply into his eyes, listening a little too intently to his words.

Clyde smoked cigars down in the basement, and the smoke, the stinking scent of them, would climb up to the main floor—and Grammy didn't even complain, didn't say a word against it, even though she wouldn't let any of her daughters' husbands smoke in the house, not even outside on the front stoop.

Grammy not keeping her hair tied up anymore while she's in the house, going to the hairdresser every week, no matter what, and getting her hair washed and curled and making sure to get that blue rinse put in once a month.

Clyde said it made her look younger.

Grammy powdering herself a little bit more heavily with the talcum—under her heavy breasts and up near her collarbones, and the white of it settling around her neck like the dust that she made sure never had more than a day's rest on her coffee table and china cabinet.

Solomon is watching all of this and the fact that Clyde is at home enough to stand over the stove, lifting the tops off the pots, sniffing and dipping his spoon in the soups and stews and gravys, tasting and then suggesting, "Maybe a bit more salt, Edna?"

"It's been more than six months. When he going?" Solomon ventures quietly, softly so as not to upset Grammy.

"Oh, Solomon," Grammy breathes and waves her hand at him before calling down to Clyde that dinner is ready, that there's ice cream and cake for dessert.

Solomon just smirks.

Donovan adores Clyde because the man makes time for him.

He takes him to play stickball in the park and to the corner store for candy and soda while Solomon is at work or locked away in his bedroom, sipping from the bottle he sneaks in every day under his arm.

Sometimes after school Donovan gathers his plastic toy soldiers and descends the stairs to Clyde's place in the basement, and they arrange the soldiers across that indoor-outdoor carpet and play war games until Grammy calls them up for dinner.

Clyde calls Donovan Cappy and Donovan refers to him as General Clyde, and they make explosive noises with their mouths, and Donovan sprays the soldiers and that indoor-outdoor carpet with spit when he tries to imitate the sound of a machine gun.

And whether Donovan wins the war game or not, Clyde rewards him, inviting him to dip his hand into the crystal bowl that's full of the peppermints Clyde loves so much.

And sometimes before Donovan scrambles up the stairs, he hugs Clyde tight around the waist and says, "Thanks," or "I love you."

The soft young skin, the scent of them, clean or not, drove him crazy.

He loved to watch them, all of them, male and female, as they moved up and down the street, playing games that children play.

He beckoned to them, enticing them with candy, money, or both.

He'd been able to touch some, able to get even further with others. "Show me," he'd say, and many did.

"Can I?" he inquired, and he would reach a steady hand out to touch a pair of young nipples.

"They're beautiful," he'd say, and bend to kiss them. "I love you," he'd mumble, and his hands would lift them up and into his lap. "See mine," he'd state, and lift his T-shirt. "You can touch them, if you want to," he'd breathe, and guide their hands.

He'd had penises in his mouth, young supple organs that quivered against his tongue, and he'd lain between the legs of babes.

"Don't cry," he'd whisper, "Don't cry, I love you."

None of them told. Not one. They wouldn't, couldn't—they were as much at fault as he was. Just as dirty. He'd convinced them that they were.

"What would your mama think if you told her about what you let me do to you?"

That's all he had to say. Those words were like glue on their lips.

Some got sick, though. Took to bed or just stopped talking altogether. One got pregnant. That had been a surprise; he thought he was sterile.

It had been so easy for so long. Little girls and little boys were much more exciting than women. He could have them do anything, anything at all, and they never asked for anything in return.

He kept a pocket full of peppermints. It was the peppermints that endeared him to them to begin with, the peppermints that got him alone with them, and the peppermints were what he left them with when he was done touching their young bodies and twisting their minds into knots.

Peppermints are what those children would think of when they were adults whenever their lovers reached out to them and they found themselves unable to respond.

On that day before Donovan's birthday, something dark and lonely was playing on the turntable. Music that reminded Donovan that his mother was gone for good. The divorce papers had come in the mail just yesterday, and now he supposed that his father would weep in the shower every day and not just on Thursdays and every other Sunday when he went for Elaine and Daisy wouldn't even take the time to say hello to him.

Tree leaves limp with heat and lack of water (it hadn't rained for three weeks) threatened to let go of their branches, even though autumn was weeks and weeks away.

The sunflowers, their petals beginning to brown and dry at the tips, wept over the wire fences, and the blacktopped street began to sweat and melt.

Inside, Donovan lay in his bed, flat on his back, dressed only in his undershorts.

"If you stay still, you'll stay cool," Grammy had advised before walking out the door. "Your father and I will be back soon. Clyde is here if you need anything," she said before dabbing at the moisture around her hairline and above her lip.

"You sure you don't want to come along?" Solomon had asked as he wiped at his neck and sideburns with the handkerchief he kept in his back pocket.

"Nah," Donovan said. "I'll just stay here."

"Just stay upstairs. Don't bother Mr. Walker," Solomon said before pulling the door closed.

The sound of the firecrackers, that and the slow sad music climbing up from the basement and some little girl outside on the sidewalk singing "Over the Rainbow," made the intense heat seem even more unbearable.

He decided that he would go downstairs and see Clyde, even though his father had told him not to.

It was cooler down there.

"Coolest part of the house." He'd heard Grammy say it on more than one occasion. He needed to be where it was cool, away from the firecrackers and that damn song that that little girl seemed to know only three verses of.

It's dark down there, darker than usual. Clyde didn't even have on the small lamp that was shaped like a naked woman.

Donovan hesitated when he reached the last step; he didn't much like the dark, and the music that was playing, the person who was singing, seemed to give the darkness an even more sinister feel.

"General," he whispered, and grasped hold of the banister. "Clyde," he called, and backed up one step.

The air was drenched with cigar smoke, and Donovan felt his chest tighten. The woman on the record hit a high note, and to Donovan it sounded like a wail—and he thought that maybe him being there wasn't a good idea at all.

He backed up another step.

"Cappy!" The voice sailed from a black corner of the basement, and the fear that gripped Donovan slipped.

"Hey, Cappy, where you been all day, boy?"

Clyde's voice was light and loose.

"Just upstairs," Donovan responded as he took a step down and squinted into the darkness.

"Well, come on in." Clyde laughed and struck a match.

The small flickering flame distorted his features, and Donovan felt his breath catch in his throat.

The look on Donovan's face made Clyde laugh, and he reached over and flicked on the lamp. "Did you bring your toys?"

There was a bottle of Scotch sitting on a crate besides the old armchair he sat in. A bottle of Scotch and one of the jelly glasses Donovan had started collecting.

"Hey, that's mine," Donovan chirped, and stepped down off the stairs.

"What?" Clyde said, and his face was his again. "This?" he asked, and lifted the glass. "Oh, Cappy, do you mind?"

Donovan thought about it for a moment. "Nah, I guess not."

"Well, you shouldn't. Friends share things, don't they?"

"I guess so," Donovan said, and moved closer. Was that the one with Scooby-Doo and Shaggy? Why, that was his favorite one.

"They do. I share things with you, don't I?"

Donovan sucked on the inside of his cheeks before responding. "Yeah."

"Well, then you shouldn't mind sharing things with me," Clyde said, and lifted the glass to his mouth and drained its contents.

"So you have a birthday tomorrow, huh?" Clyde said as he unscrewed the top from the Scotch bottle. "How old are you going to be?"

"Nine," Donovan said, as he watched the liquor spill into his favorite glass.

"Nine? Why I don't ever remember being nine." Clyde laughed and put the glass to his lips.

Donovan smiled and eased himself down onto the indoor-outdoor carpet. The stiff fibers poked through his shorts, pricking the skin of his bottom. His face contorted, and he slipped his hand beneath his butt.

"Nine. Oh, to be nine again," Clyde sang, and tipped the glass to his mouth again.

"You said you don't remember being nine," Donovan said, and then gave him a sideways glance.

Clyde laughed. "Did you bring your toys? The soldiers?"

Donovan twisted on his hands. "Nah."

"Well, don't you want to play?"

"I dunno."

Clyde tipped the bottle again.

"Who's that singing?" Donovan ventured.

"Oh, that," Clyde's eyes rolled around in his head, and then a wide smile consumed his face. "That there is Nina Simone."

"Oh." Donovan had thought it was a man.

They remained quiet through two songs, Clyde's eyes opening and closing. His head swaying back and forth in time to the music.

"Hey, those are some fine shorts you got there. Who's that on them?" Clyde asked, pointing to the cartoon figure that scaled his way across Donovan's shorts.

Donovan looked down. "Spider-Man."

"Oh, Spider-Man. He, uhm, is he on the inside, too?" Clyde's voice dropped a bit.

"What?" Donovan didn't understand.

Clyde had to make two attempts to pull himself up from the chair, and then he walked a crooked line over to Donovan.

"Well, you know Spider-Man seems to be everywhere. Is he inside the shorts, too, or just on the outside?"

Donovan pulled on his bottom lip. He wasn't sure about that.

"Well?" Clyde said, and slowly lowered himself down to one wobbly knee.

"I don't know," Donovan said, and pulled at the waistband of his shorts to see.

"Yeah, yeah," Clyde said, and leaned forward on his hands. "Let me see, Cappy," he said, and licked his lips.

Donovan looked into the old ragged face of Clyde Walker. His eyes were bulging and red, and his face was covered in a thin film of moisture even though the basement was the coolest place in the house, Grammy had said so herself.

"Well," Donovan started, but Clyde was already slipping his index finger inside Donovan's waistband, pulling the fabric away from Donovan's stomach and peering down inside. "Uh-huh. I can't tell, can you?"

Donovan looked down and then back up into Clyde's eyes. "No," he mumbled.

"Yeah, well maybe you should pull them down so that we could both see."

There was something definitely wrong here, but Donovan didn't know what exactly.

"Stand up, Cappy. Stand up so we can see."

Donovan pushed himself to his feet. His crotch came level with Clyde's face.

Clyde rocked on his one old knee and reached out to Donovan for balance. "Help the ol' General up, Cappy."

Donovan grabbed hold of Clyde's hand and pulled him to his feet.

"Thanks, Cappy," Clyde said, and patted Donovan on the head. "Let's move over to the light so that we can see better, okay?"

Donovan felt like he should leave, but instead he followed Clyde over to the lamp. Clyde touched his shoulders, a light squeeze and then another pat on the head before he came around him and eased himself back down into the chair.

He picked the bottle up and poured the last of the Scotch into the glass, and Nina Simone began to sing in a language Donovan had never heard before.

"Well, go on," Clyde said after he'd drained the glass and set it back down on the crate and folded his hands neatly in his lap.

Donovan shrugged his shoulders and turned his head toward the stairs. It was suddenly too cool in the basement.

"You need help?"

Donovan didn't say a word. He wanted to walk to the stairs so badly, his feet began to shuffle.

Clyde grabbed his hand and gently pulled him closer. "What's wrong, Cappy? You embarrassed?"

Donovan nodded his head without looking at Clyde. Tears were beginning to well up in his eyes.

"You shouldn't be," Clyde said, and stroked Donovan's fingers. "You should never be embarrassed with me," he purred.

Donovan blinked back the tears.

Clyde reached out and with his index and middle finger pulled apart the opening at the front of Donovan's shorts.

"I see your little man, Cappy," Clyde laughed. "Well, it's not so little now, is it?" he said as he pushed his finger through and poked at Donovan's penis.

Donovan's body jerked, and a tear escaped and crept its way down his cheek.

Clyde's heart skipped a beat as he took a deep breath and moved his hand to the waistband of Donovan's shorts. Carefully, gently, he pulled them down from around his waist. When the waistband hit the top of his buttocks, Clyde pulled his right hand away for a moment, in order to wipe at the saliva that was gathering at the corner of his mouth.

He sucked in air and pulled the shorts down the rest of the way, until they lay gathered on top of the boy's feet.

"N-Nooo," Donovan whimpered, and tried to back away from Clyde.

"Oh, c'mon, Cappy. You don't have to be ashamed. I won't tell anyone what you did," Clyde whispered, and pulled Donovan closer to him.

Clyde's face pressed against Donovan's chest. His steamy breath wafted around Donovan's face, and the boy's stomach began to turn. Clyde grabbed hold of his penis.

"Don't worry, I won't tell your father and Grammy what you did. You won't get in trouble 'cause I ain't gonna say a word," he said as he stroked Donovan's organ. "I won't say a word," he said again, his words hushed and shaky.

He pulled Donovan closer and then tilted his head up and kissed Donovan on the mouth.

Donovan recoiled, but Clyde held him tight and then pushed his tongue between Donovan's lips.

Donovan thought he would puke.

With his free hand, Clyde hurriedly unzipped his pants and slipped his hand down between his legs.

The music's melancholy strain swelled, but not loud enough to drown out Clyde's gasps and moans as he caressed himself and Donovan, and somewhere outside, the little girl's song came to an abrupt halt. The room exploded with sadness just as Clyde shuddered and fell limp against him.

He didn't touch himself for a long time after Clyde. Didn't even want to hold his penis when he pissed. Wrapped his wash-cloth around it when he had to, sometimes just sat down on the toilet like a woman, so as not to have to bother with it at all.

Donovan had spent the better part of that year avoiding Clyde. Sometimes when he looked at the old man, he thought that maybe he had dreamed the whole thing up.

Maybe the heat had been too much for him and he had hallu-cinated the whole thing. Because when it was over, when his hand finally let go of Donovan's penis, the room seemed to be brighter.

Not only was the lamp on, but so was the main light, and the music had changed; James Brown was singing by then. The bot-tle was gone, and so was the jelly glass, and Donovan was seated back down on the indoor-outdoor carpet, Clyde in his chair, sucking on a peppermint and flipping through a comic book.

"This is the same cartoon on your briefs, Cappy," he said, and held up the Spider-Man comic book so he could see.

Grammy was calling down to him from upstairs, and the rustling of brown paper bags could be heard as his father removed the contents and placed them in the refrigerator and cupboards.

It all had seemed like a dream then, and Donovan had stood up and even waved good-bye to Clyde before starting slowly up the stairs. He wasn't sure, not sure at all what had just happened, but his penis did feel odd between his legs now, like it didn't belong there at all.

Clyde had waved back and then said, "Don't worry Cappy. It's just between us."

Clyde died a year after that. Dropped dead in an X-rated movie theater on Forty-second Street, and the police called Grammy. Her name and number were on a tiny slip of paper they found tucked in his wallet behind a playing card that had a picture of a naked Asian girl who couldn't have been more that thirteen years old. The cops had passed the card around. Some laughed at it and shook their heads, while others turned their mouths down in disgust.

The state had to bury him. He didn't have an insurance policy, and the court suit he had with the city—the one he made sure to mention every single day since he first moved in there—why, that didn't exist at all.

Donovan didn't want to go to the funeral, tried to pretend to be sick, but Grammy had caught him watching a karate flick on television and jumping about like some Mexican jumping bean imitating Bruce Lee.

"You ain't sick, boy," she'd yelled, and tugged on his ear and then popped him upside his head.

It had all come back to him then. Like a rush of cold water, it came. Just as he looked down into the dead face of Clyde Walker. The music, the heat, and Clyde's hands—pulling on his penis, kissing on his neck and lips.

He heard him for the first time that day, heard his voice in his head as if he were alive and well and standing right behind him instead of lying dead in the casket.

Nice to see you again, Cappy!

Donovan had jerked at the sound of his voice, and then leaned over and spit right into Clyde's dead black face.

Grammy didn't move for a moment. She just stood there with her mouth open, her eyes blinking, and then her hand came up and she slapped Donovan down to the floor.

"What the hell has gotten into you, boy?" Grammy bellowed, forgetting she was in a funeral home and people were mourning.

Donovan didn't have an explanation. He just rubbed at his stinging cheek and gave her a blank stare.

Ages Thirteen to Fifteen

The years that followed Clyde's death had been unhappy and turbulent ones for Donovan.

His teachers called constantly and sent notes home to complain about Donovan's moodiness, his downright rudeness and uncontrollable temper.

Grammy blamed it on Daisy.

Solomon said, "Well, all boys fight," to the junior high school principal, who was a heavyset man who stood a good six feet five inches. He looked like a football player and as if he'd had a few good fights in his lifetime.

"Yes, they do," the principal said. "I've got three sons of my own, and I myself was thirteen a long time ago. Yes, they do fight. But we still don't condone it," he said, and then stretched his arms across his chest and locked his fingers together. "But your son, he doesn't just fight—he brawls. He's unmerciful, and I believe potentially murderous."

The man had spoken those words so calmly, so matter-of-factly, that Solomon wasn't sure he had heard right, and a small laugh escaped him. But the principal wasn't laughing, nor was he smiling.

"What?" Solomon said, and cleared his throat. The tape recorder in his mind had just played back what the principal said. "Murderous?" Solomon said, and then he sucked his teeth and shook his head. "That's a strong word. You're exaggerating." Solomon laughed, hoping the principal was putting him on.

"No, I'm not kidding. I think your son needs help."

"Help?"

"Therapy."

"A shrink?"

"A therapist. Psychiatrist, maybe."

"Oh, what kind of bullshit—?"

"Mr. Barrows, please don't curse at me."

Solomon was getting mad. He had a slow temper, but this man was pushing him. He should have let Grammy come in and handle it. He didn't need this bullshit, wasn't anything wrong with his son, except . . .

"Well, his mother left him, and . . ." The whole story was out and on the table before Solomon even knew what he was saying.

The principal just nodded his head and listened. "Well, it might be a good idea for, um, both of you to get some therapy," the principal said as he slid the box of tissues across the desk to Solomon.

In Grammy's eyes, all Donovan's problems began and ended with Daisy.

"You let him spend too much time with her," Grammy had said to Solomon. "He's confused. You carting him between here and *her*."

"I-It is his m-mother, Grammy."

Grammy had given Solomon a disgusted look before slamming

the spoon down on the stove. "I know she's his mother. That's not my fault. That was *your* choice, not mine." Grammy grabbed the spoon again and then added, "You just remember that."

Solomon said nothing.

"I just think that until he's a little older it would be best if he just sees her once every other week instead of every weekend."

Solomon nodded thoughtfully.

Grammy stirred the chili before continuing. "That man she's got—"

Solomon cringed.

"—what do you know about him? He could be some type of lunatic or drug dealer. That girl ain't picky about who she chooses to lay up with—"

Solomon grimaced.

"—just like a bitch, let any old mutt climb on top of her."

Solomon dropped his head into his hands and began to rock. Grammy slammed the spoon down on the stove again. "Solomon, are you listening to me!"

Solomon jumped. "Y-Yes, ma'am."

"Now I know Donovan is close to his sister, and I don't mind having her here, even though she's a willful little thing." Grammy chewed on her bottom lip and looked thoughtfully at the ceiling. "If I had her long enough, I would break her little behind out of that," she mumbled under her breath.

"Huh?" Solomon said.

Grammy waved her hands at him. "Nothing, nothing. We gonna have to get that boy involved in something. Weekend stuff—that'll keep him around here on weekends instead of uptown."

Solomon gave his mother a doubtful glance.

Grammy twisted her mouth and barked, "You want your son calling some other man daddy, boy!"

Solomon dropped his eyes and shook his head.

High school was painful enough, but Grammy had gone and enrolled him at the Boys Club, had made him take up tennis and swimming, volleyball and chess, filling up all his weekend time, leaving almost no time at all to spend with his mother and sister.

He was fourteen by then, long and lanky with feet that stuck a mile out in front of him, tripping him up whenever they got a chance. His voice cracked and failed him at the most inopportune times, and not one hair had thought to push out on his chin to steal the attention away from the acne that covered his face like bee stings.

He preferred his own company, and had little to do with people outside his family. A chronic masturbator, he didn't even make eye contact with any of the young girls who giggled and laughed their way through classes and fifth-period lunch. But he thought about them later while he was in the shower or alone at night in bed.

It disgusted him, how often he found himself doing it. He thought he must be sick, that this thing he did to himself must be some type of aftereffect of Clyde (because sometimes he could hear Clyde's voice egging him on), and he worried that touching himself might lead to touching someone else in that way, the way Clyde had touched him.

By tenth grade, things had gotten a little better. He'd convinced Grammy to let him drop chess and tennis. Volleyball followed; he kept the swimming and picked up basketball.

He became more comfortable with his peers, and his acne began retreating, his body grew into his feet, and before the school year was over he'd been absorbed by a group of boys who talked a lot about sex and beating their meat, and Donovan was relieved to find out that it was normal.

His grades and conduct improved, and he went out for the school basketball team and found that he was quite good.

But his fears bubbled in his throat when it came to the locker room. Donovan was careful about where his eyes fell when he disrobed, vigilant about keeping his head focused on his hands and the soap he held when he showered. Laughed at the dirty jokes that got tossed around in the steam, but never let his eyes move far from the white tiled walls and silver showerhead.

The girls started to pay more attention to him. Batting their eyes when he was nearby, slapping his arm and laughing, even though he knew he hadn't said anything funny.

His friend Brian McCall gave Donovan's number to a few girls who inquired about him. When they called and asked for Donovan—Don as he was known in school—Grammy's mouth would twist up, and she would make sure she banged the phone down on the table a few times before calling Donovan to the phone.

"Girls at that age are the worst. They get boys into a whole heap of trouble, ya hear? You watch yourself and keep your *thing* in your pants," Grammy said even before Donovan had a chance to cover the receiver with his palm.

Grammy made sure she remained close by, pretending to clean or knit while she eavesdropped on what Donovan was saying on the phone. "Okay boy," she'd interrupt soon after Donovan said hello and how ya doing? "Don't be tying up my phone line, hear? You got ten minutes left."

She wouldn't lose Donovan the way she lost Homer and Solomon.

No way, no how.

Ages Sixteen to Eighteen

He still hadn't done it. Slept with a girl. "Popped their cherry," as Brian put it. Brian had done it all, "Finger fucked, doggy-style, sixty-nine." He listed them out for Donovan as they sat on the floor in his room at Grammy's, watching the Celtics take the Hornets.

They were both dressed in T-shirts and sweatpants and cradled half-empty Sprite bottles in their hands. A box with four cold slices of pizza lay open on top of the bed, and the room smelled, "God-awful," Grammy had said when she peeked in to check on them. "Feet, funk, and sweat. Pee-u!" She laughed and slammed the door.

"Sadeena sucked my dick," Brian said between the gulps of soda.

Donovan grabbed the basketball and began tossing it up into the air. He'd never even kissed a girl, and he was going on sixteen. "Dang," he muttered.

"Almost sucked it clean off." Brian laughed and slapped the ball from Donovan's reach.

The basketball hit the wall over the dresser and dropped onto the clutter of schoolbooks and magazines that was piled there.

"No ball-playing in the house!" Grammy screamed up from below them.

Brian and Donovan just rolled their eyes.

Donovan wasn't quite sure he believed everything Brian told him. Some of his stories seemed far-fetched for a fifteen-year-old. He claimed his first sexual experience was when he was ten, with his baby-sitter. "Big titties, fat ass." That's how Brian described her.

"How about you, man, when was your first time?"

With me, Cappy. Tell him that your first time was with me.

Donovan shook his head vehemently, clearing his mind of Clyde's voice and the dark time in the basement.

"Same thing, man," he lied, and shifted his eyes down to his sneaker. "'Cept my baby-sitter had small titties and a big ass."

They'd laughed long and hard about it.

By junior year Donovan had become quite popular. His arms and legs had grown muscular, a thin mustache settled above his top lip and a thatch of dark hair at his chin. His voice cavernous, and the girls had much to say about his close-cut curls. "Good hair," they whispered, and sometimes even got close enough to touch it.

He was the top scorer on the basketball team, was maintaining a straight-A average in four of his seven classes, and someone had even suggested he go out for senior class president the following year.

The girls flocked to him during lunch and after school. They enjoyed his earnestness, the kindness he showed to both the pretty and not-so-pretty girls. Donovan was just an all-around nice guy.

The phone calls increased, and so did Grammy's frustration. "You got a lot going for you; don't let none of these little hot-ass girls ruin it for you," Grammy screeched each time Donovan dashed to the phone, yelling, "It's for me!"

Collegiate scouts came to watch him play. Him and his best friend, Brian, the hottest things on the court. They were written up in *Amsterdam News* and dubbed MVP by their coach.

Brian used his small fame to his advantage. "Tail, tail, and more tail," is what Brian would whisper in his ears whenever they left a game and a throng of young women rushed them at the player's entrance.

Donovan didn't take advantage of any of it. Grammy had warned him good and even nodded over at his father, who sat slumped and sad on the couch, "See what can happen if you're not careful," she said, not caring that she was talking about Donovan's mother.

Some girls, the bold ones, the type Donovan was sure Grammy was always referring to, would show up on his front stoop and ring the bell. Grammy always got to the door before he did. Donovan was never expecting anyone.

"Yes?" Grammy would say, and smile sweetly.

"Hello, may I please speak to Donovan?" they would say with a large bright smile plastered across their face.

"Who are you?" Grammy would ask, and cock her head to one side. Still smiling, still sweet.

The names tumbled forth, and Grammy kept smiling, all the while noticing the nail polish, makeup, the clothing—too tight, too revealing, and too loud in color.

She summed them up right there on her stoop, summed them

up and decided that they were not good enough for her grandson, not at all.

"Your mama know you over here looking for a boy?" she'd
ask them, the smile replaced with a sneer. "You should be home
with your head in a book."

The girls, their smile would waver and then crumble altogether before their eyes dropped down to their shoes. Some
spoke up, said, "My mother know where I'm at." Or, "Ma'am, I
am a straight-A student and—"

Grammy stepped out onto the stoop and pulled the door up
closed behind her. The girls, they were granted with a full view of
Grammy, and always took a small step backwards.

"You sassing me, girl?" Grammy would exclaim, and rest her
hands on her hips.

Sometimes there was a reply, other times just the quick flutter
of lashes and the hurried sound of shoe sole against pavement as
the girl moved double time away from the porch.

Ages Eighteen to Twenty-one

What's on his mind by the time he's enrolled in his first year of college has replaced playing basketball.

What's on his mind sits close by in Biology and behind him in Art class. He's a first-year freshman, and she, a junior.

Her skin is dark and as smooth as glass, and try as he does, he can't find a blemish on her. Her hair is cut close to her head, and while that could be a problem (Grammy said women should wear their hair like women, not like men), her smile makes up for it, that and the laughter that reminds him of the soca music his Antiguan roommate plays on Friday nights when he mixes up batches of rum punch.

Her name is Sylvia, and he figures it must translate into something beautiful, because that's what she is.

When he finally gets up the nerve to talk to her, it's close to Thanksgiving and they find that there are just two years between them, and that she is the product of a divorce and once lived in

Brooklyn, but now resides in the Bronx with her father and his new wife.

They go out, and he finds that she's easy to talk to and knows about sports and loves the Knicks, and he says he does, too, even though he doesn't.

She wears oils instead of perfume and big gold hoop earrings that bounce against her cheeks when she laughs. Her fingers are long and perfect; he knows this because she's all of the time covering her mouth when she laughs.

He likes her teeth, and one day he reaches for her wrist when she goes to cover her laughing mouth, and tells her so.

When he's with her he can almost totally forget about Clyde and the basement and the bad thing that happened there.

They study together, she reads to him from Shakespeare and Faulkner, and although he doesn't really get all of what the passages mean, he doesn't mind because it's the sound of her voice he craves.

Within weeks they move from library to lounge and then finally to her dorm.

There's no place to sit but the floor or the bed, and so they end up on the bed and she ends up in his arms, her head resting against his chest, her hand pulling his arm around her shoulder.

The first few times she does it, his arm feels awkward, dislodged; he looks over at it and does not even recognize it.

"What's wrong?" Sylvia asks, her face a mess of bewilderment.

Donovan just shrugs it off with a smile.

The first kiss is worse.

There is no warning, no licking of dry lips to ready, just her lips on his and her tongue in his mouth, and he practically pushes her down to the ground, and all the light that she's brought to him over the past few weeks goes gray and then black.

"S-Sorry," is all he can say when he sees the tears in her eyes and the hurt and confusion on her face.

Weeks pass and so do they, in the halls, across the campus lawn until finally he stops her and they begin again, and this time, this time he's ready for the kiss, poised for it and everything else that follows.

She's done this before. He can tell because his heart is beating so fast he can hardly catch his breath. Sylvia's face is serene, but her mouth and eyes are smiling as he fumbles with the buttons of her blouse. He's so nervous his hands tremble and he can't get her bra unhooked, so she does it for him.

She's done this before.

He wants to enjoy her body, the curve of her neck, her full breasts and flat stomach, but there are brightly colored stuffed animals everywhere, on the windowsill, bookshelf, on the floor in the corner of the room. He can't concentrate on her touch, her scent, the feel of her lips against his throat, her nipples between his fingers. He can't concentrate because the black button eyes of the animals are staring at him, and for one strange minute he thinks that Grammy is hidden somewhere among them.

Grammy told him that sex was a beautiful thing between married people. It was nastiness any other way. And in some ways it was.

Sylvia places his hand between her legs, and Donovan almost recoils. It's wet and warm there.

Donovan thinks he might be sick.

He doesn't enjoy her tongue in his mouth, her nipples are okay, but her fingers taste funny, tastes the way she . . . smells.

Her mouth's hot, and finds every bit of skin that belongs to him. He feels fire creeping down his back, spreading through his thighs, singeing his toes. His lips are moving, praying maybe or possibly begging. And when she climbs on top of him he hears Grammy in the corner of his mind reminding him to keep his thing in his pants, but Clyde's voice tells him something different.

Sylvia rides him slowly while he grips her hips and stares deep into her eyes.

Black button eyes watching you, Cappy!

Donovan hangs on, hangs on for dear life as the heat finds its way up and into his groin. He squeezes his eyes shut, and his lips stop moving, his mouth falls open, and Sylvia whimpers and kisses him, him and the tears that are streaming down his face.

He wasn't going back, not even for the spring semester.

"What about basketball?"

"Bum knee," Solomon reminded her, and tapped his own knee.

"Grammy, I haven't played since first semester, remember? I was in that soft cast for a month?" Donovan says.

Grammy looks up at the ceiling and strokes her throat. "Oh, yeah. I forgot about that," she says softly. "Well, what are you going to do, then?" Grammy asks as she bends down and peeks at the baking turkey through the clear window of the oven door.

"Work," Donovan responds, and pulls at the end of the tablecloth.

"Work?" Solomon repeats, and leans back in the chair until it totters on two legs.

"I done told you about that, Solomon," Grammy yells, and snaps the towel off Solomon's head and he hurriedly brings the chair back down on all fours.

"I thought you wanted to be an engineer or something?" he says, and then picks up the newspaper and begins to thumb through it.

"Changed my mind."

"Your cousins are all in college," Grammy says, and then finally snatches open the oven door.

"Not all of them—some of them are in jail," Donovan retorts.

"Your mother's not going to like it," Solomon says.

"Yeah, well."

"Who cares what she thinks, anyway? If Donovan don't want to go to college, he don't have to go. It's not for everyone, you know."

"What you thinking about doing?" Solomon asks, folding the top corner of the sports section and then closing the paper.

"I dunno."

"Well, you take all the time you need, and when you're ready then you go out and find something. When you're ready, no rush," Grammy says while closing the oven door and resting her hands on her hips. "It's Christmas. Holidays ain't no time to be out looking for a job. Maybe in the spring, when the weather breaks."

Solomon shakes his head, and Donovan tilts his chair backwards on two legs. Grammy just smiles.

He couldn't go back to Rutgers, not after what had gone on with Sylvia and then Lorraine.

He never really wanted them to stay. Well, it was okay for Sylvia to be there after their first time together. She held him and didn't embarrass him by asking about his tears. It was fine the second time, too. But after that he wanted to be alone afterwards.

He liked waking up alone, satisfied with the scent they left lingering on his pillow, although none too happy with the wet spot on the sheets.

But they always insisted on staying, and he had to pretend to be comfortable with them pressed up against his chest, their hair in his face, and their arms curled like snakes around him, pulling him across their naked breasts.

It happened the fifth time Sylvia stayed with him. He opened his eyes to find her huddled in the corner, shaking and crying, students outside his room banging on his door and someone screaming for security.

Evidently he'd had a bad dream. A violent dream, so violent he'd sat straight up in the bed, punching at the air and kicking wildly with his feet.

It had been embarrassing. "Nightmares," he'd laughed.

Me, Clyde's voice rang around him.

But Sylvia was inconsolable and had gathered her things and marched off to her dormitory and the safety of her own bed.

They'd seen each other a few more times after that, but she'd finally broken it off before graduating the following spring.

Lorraine hadn't been a girlfriend, but they always seemed to find each other after keg parties and on Friday nights when he'd smoked too much marijuana.

It had happened with her, too, and she had been low enough to spread it around campus.

He couldn't face anyone after she told. He imagined that every snicker, every guffaw or whispered conversation was being had at his expense.

He didn't need this, not any of it, and so packed up in the middle of the winter semester and returned home, where life was safe and predictable.

He'd always been able to talk to Daisy about things. Things that Grammy scoffed at or gave him a lecture about.

He hadn't shared his first time with his mother, but had called her in a panic three months later when he thought he'd *gotten something*.

He could never share that with Grammy. In her mind he was still her sweet little virgin grandson. And Solomon was a whole different story; he'd started hitting the bottle pretty heavy over the last few years and had taken to spending most of his time locked away in his bedroom watching reruns.

The something turned out to be gonorrhea, and Daisy hadn't even yelled at him. She just told him that he needed to be more selective about who he slept with and then marched him straight to the corner drugstore and bought him enough condoms to last him a year.

Now he was sitting in his mother's spacious Harlem apartment telling her that he was quitting school.

"Well, there must be a reason why you want to drop out?"

Donovan pushed his palms across the gleaming mahogany table and allowed his eyes to focus on the plants that were lined up against the wall.

"I just don't think it's for me," he mumbled.

Elaine was seated next to Donovan, picking at the nail polish on her fingers. Daisy considered her for a moment and then turned her attention back to Donovan.

"Baby, if you don't like the school, you can go somewhere else, you know?"

She was disappointed with him. He could tell by the slow and even way she spoke to him.

"Stop that, Elaine."

Elaine immediately lowered her hands into her lap.

Donovan dropped his eyes and pushed his palm again across the dining room table. "I just don't want to go anymore."

Elaine, who looked so much like her mother, turned doe eyes on Daisy and stuck her bottom lip out. "He doesn't want to go anymore, Mom."

Daisy shook her head and stifled a laugh. This was supposed to be a serious moment.

"Well, Donovan, what are you going to do with your life, then?"

Elaine looked up at her big brother and waited.

Donovan had no idea what he was going to do after tomorrow, much less the rest of his life. "Well," he began, and pulled his palm back across the table. "Grammy said—"

Daisy's whole demeanor crumbled. She cocked her head to one side, leaned back in her chair, and folded her hands across her chest. Elaine just shook her head at Donovan's stupidity.

"That's your grandmother, Donovan, but you know I don't want you to share anything with me that has rolled out of that woman's mouth."

Daisy's feathers were rustled, and her milky complexion went beet red.

Donovan swallowed and began again. "What I meant to say was that I'm going to fill out some applications with the city. Maybe get on at the post office—"

Daisy bristled.

Donovan looked at Elaine before looking down at the floor. "—Or transit. Maybe."

Daisy stood up and smoothed her track pants. "Okay, okay. You've made a decision. You have a plan. I can respect that."

Donovan felt his body relax.

"We can respect that," Elaine mimicked.

There were delivery jobs, a few months of unloading boxes midnight to eight at the local Pathmark. A one-year stint driving for a Trailways bus line, and then transit finally called.

He started out as a token booth clerk. He didn't mind it too much. He met interesting people, saw bizarre things, and had plenty of time to sit and think. From there he moved to conductor and finally motorman.

He liked being a motorman most of all. Enjoyed barreling

through the narrow dark tunnels and the solitary silence of his booth.

Clyde hardly ever found him there beneath the city streets, and on the rare occasion he did, his voice got trampled beneath the rolling steel wheels of the train.

Them

1999-2000

December

"I remember that girl," they said. "Her mother wore long red beads around her neck, wrapped her head up in colorful scarves, used the same scarves as skirts, smoked weed, and burned scented candles. Men came and went. Came and went.

"The lovebirds? Did you ever see them? They were always huddled together; one move and so did the other. I guess that's why they call them lovebirds, huh?

"She let them go after Pat, her daughter, stepped off the platform at Utica Avenue.

"No more love, she was heard to say, and stopped wearing her hair tied up. Kept the beads, though, but let the birds go.

"Kept the gold-and-white cage, too, but not her mind.

"You can see her off of Canal Street and Leonard; she's pushing a shopping cart. Can't miss her, gold-and-white birdcage and red beads."

*　　*　　*

The first collage Campbell pieced together began with that story. A sharp and painful memory that would never seem to wane or pale. It spilled from her in tears and kept her up at night, clutching her heart and rocking at the edge of her bed.

She thought she was dying, slipping away with every short breath she took. Some days her heart raced in her chest, and other times it didn't seem to want to beat at all. There were night sweats, weight loss, and dizziness. She was sure she was dying.

"You're not dying," Dr. Bing sighed, and shook his head.

Campbell was seated on the examining table, her legs dangled beneath her as she stared at the doctor's humped back.

"All of your tests came back fine." He kept his back to her as he scribbled notes down in her file. "You're just anxious, that's all."

"What?" Campbell spoke for the first time since she'd disrobed and climbed onto the table. "What did you say?"

Dr. Bing turned around, and Campbell had to resist the urge to laugh. His pale green eyes looked as large as eggs behind his bifocals.

Dr. Bing scratched at his full beard and considered Campbell for a moment before walking toward her. "You have an acute anxiety condition."

Campbell looked down at her feet. She needed a pedicure. She curled her toes. "What exactly does that mean?" she asked without looking up.

Dr. Bing sighed and reached over and pulled the chair from beneath his desk and sat down. He folded his hands and looked earnestly at Campbell. "What are you worried about?"

Campbell winced at his question. She wasn't worried about just one thing. There were hundreds of things. No, millions of things she worried about. But most of all she worried about dying empty, the way Pat had.

*   *   *

Campbell had been there when it happened.

They'd had dinner that night, all five of them. The select few that had made it out of Brookline Projects and made good. Anita, stout but beautiful, had graduated high school with honors and received a scholarship to Johnson & Wales University in Rhode Island, where she took culinary courses, married, opened a bed and breakfast, divorced and took her share of the monies made during that ten-year marriage, came back to New York and opened a restaurant.

Laverna had joined the army and had spent eight years of doing who knew what, but when she finally came back home, she was gay, but told them she had always been that way. She said her attraction to men had just been a phase.

Porsche had married her childhood sweetheart. A skinny boy named Clark who played a mean game of jacks and could jump double Dutch better than any one of them.

Campbell and Pat had been the closest of the five. They had the most in common. Both were good students, but Pat made straight As while Campbell made Bs.

Pat's mother, Alverna, had been some sort of bohemian. At least that's what Millie referred to her as. Her husband, Chuck, was killed in action while serving in Vietnam, and now the government would send her a check for the rest of her life, as long as she never remarried.

She'd lock herself in the bathroom three times a day to smoke a joint. She said she needed to do that because she missed her husband and smoking reefer took her to another plane, one that allowed her to communicate with her dead husband.

"Daddy said to tell you hello," she would say as she backed out of the bathroom, spraying Lysol with one hand and fanning the last wisps of smoke away with the other.

Alverna said that Chuck was her soul mate and that she'd never love another man as long as she lived. She'd fuck them, though, she said, because women had needs.

She believed in stuff like that—astrology, tarot cards, aliens—things that made the girls giggle and spin their index fingers near their temples when Alverna wasn't looking.

When Pat and Campbell graduated from junior high school, Alverna had given them gold pendants of penguins as gifts. "Penguins mate for life," she said, and smiled. "I hope one day the two of you will be lucky enough to find your soul mates like I did," Alverna said as a whimsical look blanketed her face.

The girls had just nodded and thanked her before walking away, believing more than ever that Alverna had a few screws loose.

Pat had made a decision that she was going to do it, to have sex with Darryl Pennington from 258 Stanley Avenue. She told all of them that she'd popped one of her mother's birth control pills and was cutting school the next day in order to do it.

Anita had been the first one of them to lose her virginity. It had been a painful ordeal with her cousin's boyfriend. Porsche and Clark had spoken about it, but Porsche was too afraid of her mother finding out and then putting her out on the street.

Campbell had already done it and was embarrassed to admit that she hadn't had sense enough to steal birth control pills or even ask Trevor if he had a rubber. So she lied and told the girls that they had used a rubber and that yeah, yeah, it had felt good.

The one birth control pill Pat had popped hadn't been enough to ward off Darryl's fifteen-year-old sperm, and the same held true for Campbell's imaginary condom—and they'd both discovered they were pregnant just as their third year of high school began.

Pat had given birth to a son and named him Tye. Campbell, a girl named Macon.

Now they had come together again as they had so many times in the past when one of their own was celebrating or suffering.

There were dark circles under her eyes, and Pat, already petite, had dropped two whole dress sizes in thirty days.

Anita shared a worried look with Campbell. Laverna and Porsche couldn't contain their surprise at Pat's condition; it marched all across their faces.

They spoke about small things, breaking bread and chipping away at the ice with trivial conversation that no one was really interested in while Pat just nodded and looked through them.

Anita drained her wineglass and gave her friends a look that told her she had had enough and placed her hand on top of Pat's and said, "Baby, what is going on with you?"

Of course, Anita knew what was going on. All of them knew. Campbell had shared it with each and every one of them. She had to; Pat wouldn't take any of their calls.

Pat smiled sadly. "Nothing. Really," she whispered, and already the tears had begun to well up in her eyes.

Laverna and Porsche sighed and shook their heads miserably.

"Pat," Anita cooed, and squeezed her hand. "Pat, baby, it's okay. It's okay."

Campbell, Laverna, and Porsche sounded agreement and nodded their heads.

"It hurt everywhere and only stops hurting when I hold my breath," Pat blubbered. "I wish I could hold my breath forever," she cried.

Nearby diners looked on, and one woman even dabbed the corner of her eyes. Campbell felt her chest heave. Porsche took a deep cleansing breath, and Laverna looked away and cleared her throat.

Hadn't they all been there? Not just hurt by a man, not their hearts simply broken, but bludgeoned?

Some how the *He ain't worth it. He did you a favor*, and *You deserve betters* just didn't seem appropriate this time around.

Anita pulled Pat to her, holding her close while her body quaked with sobs. All four of them had taken turns hugging her, telling her that they loved her and always would. Reminding her that it would be okay . . . maybe not today or even fifty days from then, but that it would, one day.

"Sorry." Pat apologized the four blocks they walked to the train station.

Anita had told them they could stay overnight at her Upper East Side apartment, but both Pat and Campbell had declined. Laverna had driven into the city, but she was living in Parkchester, and even though she said she would drive them back to Brooklyn, Campbell thought that was putting her too far out of her way and would not hear of it.

Porsche had a place in Chelsea, just four blocks from the restaurant. She hugged Pat extra hard and told her she would call her the next day and that she'd better answer the phone. She kissed her quickly on the cheek before hugging Campbell and shooting out across the avenue just as the traffic light went from green to red.

They'd decided to take the train.

It was late, and there were only four or five other people on the platform. Every breath, utterance or shuffling of feet echoed around them and made the cold night seem even more bitter.

There were plenty of empty seats, but Pat chose to sit next to a little boy and his mother. Campbell shrugged her shoulders and slid into an empty seat across from them.

Pat smiled down at the little boy. "Don't he remind you of Tye when he was that age?" she asked Campbell without looking at her.

Campbell considered the little boy. He did resemble Tye a little bit. "Yeah, he does," she said.

"Tye is almost a man. He's with his father now more than he is with me," she said, her eyes swinging between the little boy and Campbell. "If I went away . . . he would be okay without me now," she said, and reached out and stroked the little boy's hand.

The mother smiled a little nervously and pulled her son closer to her side.

"What are you talking about?" Campbell said, leaning forward and giving the woman a reassuring smile.

"I feel so empty," Pat said.

Campbell made a face. "What?"

"Nothing," Pat sighed and slumped back against the seat.

The train roared through the tunnels, and Campbell slipped into and out of sleep, her eyes rolling open every so often and falling on Pat's troubled face.

When they stepped off the train at Utica Avenue, the December wind had found its way down into the tunnel, and outside a light snow had started to fall.

Two A trains came and went, and Campbell and Pat had not spoken a word to each other.

Fifteen minutes passed, and Campbell balanced herself along the yellow line at the edge of the platform and leaned over to peer down the dimly lit subway tunnel.

A train was coming, but not on that track. "Dammit, another A train," Campbell complained under her breath, and turned to suggest to Pat that they brave the cold instead, but Pat was gone.

Campbell's head swung left and then right, and there was Pat, walking down the platform, head down, hands stuffed deep into her pockets.

"Pat!" Campbell called to her. "I think there's a problem with the local," she said, and started across the platform. "Let's try to get a cab."

It was, Campbell would remember, like a movie in slow motion.

The front of the train coming around the bend, one headlight out and the other bright and white. The sound of the wheels screeching as they hugged the tracks, the tired look on the motorman's face and the cigarette hanging from the corner of his mouth.

The slow turn of Pat's head and the jerky awkward movement the body makes when the mind has made a sudden decision.

She stepped right off the platform, right in front of the train.

The shock of it all made Campbell laugh, because there was Pat, arms and legs spread wide like wings, plastered against the front of the train like a cartoon character, before her body flew off and was crushed beneath the iron wheels.

The train squealed and then came to a stop, and Campbell thought that it was odd that the train still sounded as if the motorman was riding the brakes, odd that the doors were open and people were getting off and giving her peculiar stares and still the screeching continued, odd she thought until she was up and out on the street, trying hard to get away from that sound and finally realizing that the sound was coming from her.

Campbell had taken Pat's suicide hard. She and the rest of their friends, Anita, Laverna and Porsche, had held each other and wept over the closed casket that held Pat's body.

For days Campbell kept forgetting she was gone, picking up the telephone to call Pat to share some piece of good news or gossip.

Everything suddenly seemed too complicated, too cramped.

Campbell spent a week cleaning out closets, lining and rearranging drawers while Macon and Millie watched but stayed out of her way, and allowing her grief to work its way through her.

When she finally took a moment to look at herself in the mirror, she saw the dark circles under her eyes, the mess of hair on her head. She would have to do something about that woman looking back at her; she would have to make some changes there, too.

Campbell left early one morning and came back home with her hair in a mass of twists that looked like worms to Millie.

"What is that?" Millie asked, pointing at Campbell's head.

"Locks. Dreadlocks."

"Oh," Millie sounded. "Like the Jamaicans wear?"

"Yeah."

"Oh." Millie sounded again. "You going to be one of those Rasta people now?"

"No."

"It looks great, Mom," Macon said, jumping to her mother's defense.

Millie just shrugged her shoulders. She hoped it was just a phase.

Dr. Bing waited for Campbell to answer.

"Yes, I guess I'm worried about a lot of things. My daughter, my family—" She stopped to take a breath and then continued with a little laugh. "—the state of the world."

Dr. Bing did not laugh with her, but nodded his head thoughtfully. "I'm going to prescribe some Paxil for you," he said, and reached behind him to grab a prescription pad off his desk. "It'll help you rest and, well—" He paused to scribble down the dosage. "—not be so anxious."

Campbell chewed on her lips and looked around the room.

Dr. Bing ripped the prescription from the pad and held it out to her. "If you like, I can refer you to a—"

Campbell's body went rigid as she predicted the next word to roll off his mouth.

"—Psychologist."

Campbell swallowed.

"Are you involved in any activities?" Dr. Bing pulled at his beard and looked down at the floor as he thought about his next set of words. "Uhm, clubs, associations . . . church?"

No, no and no again, Campbell thought to herself. It was just work and home most days. She shook her head.

Dr. Bing nodded. "Well, you need to involve yourself in something, something time-consuming and distracting."

Campbell nodded her head.

"I'm going to write down the name and number of the psychologist." He began scribbling on the prescription pad. "Just in case what I'm prescribing and suggesting doesn't work."

Belly dancing class with Macon, the department softball team, knitting. She'd tried those things and dozens more. The pills were helping some, she did manage to get five hours of sleep instead of the usual two, and the night sweats had stopped. But during the day, the pills made her feel lethargic and dull minded.

The idea came to mind while she was writing in her journal. As a child, she'd always enjoyed making collages, had loved the smell of the glue and the sense the scattered pictures came together to create.

The collage had come together in bits and pieces of color and black-and-white images from magazines and newspapers. Images that represented who Pat had been and the person she'd hoped to become.

It had started slowly, a ruby-colored heart fractured at its center. Large brown eyes brimming with tears, a mother holding her son, a white picket fence, calla lilies, a hope chest, doves.

Campbell worked at it feverishly without knowing exactly

what it was she was doing, not even aware that the grief was draining away from her, the constant fear subsiding.

Millie saw it happening, and so did Macon—and they'd both breathed a sigh of relief and thanked the Lord that that particular storm was finally passing.

When the collage was done, Campbell's fingertips crusted and white with glue, she stood back to examine what she'd put together.

Entries from her journal, printed in black letters on a small white rectangular piece of paper, sat at its middle, the clipped images, some with jagged edges, others with perfect corners or rounded borders, were assembled around it, covering the entire thirty-by-twenty-four-inch piece of board.

Something inside her whispered thank you, and for the first time in months Campbell smiled instead of wept.

On the night Pat stepped off the platform. Donovan was in a bar, eavesdropping. He did that sometimes.

The bar was empty for a Friday night. He supposed it was due to the cold. Better for him—he could eat his French fries and burger in peace. The game was on the mounted thirty-six-inch above his head.

But his mind wasn't focused on his food or the game. The two guys that had come in behind him, the two guys that had started out with Heinekens and were now on their second whiskey and water, were talking about a letter one had received in the mail.

"Man, she started out with I love you and I want you and all of that why can't we be together shit and the baby needs you—," the man said.

Some women just don't know how to let go, Donovan thought.

"She got a child with you?" the friend asked.

"She pregnant now."

"Damn."

Should have kept your dick covered up, Donovan laughed to himself.

"You know what I'm saying? She wanna trap a brother. I told her, I got three kids already—"

"Thought you just had the two?"

"Well, Lamont ain't mine, but I helps out, you know?"

"Uh-huh."

"So like I was saying, I told her, I said look here, I ain't trying to be a bastard or something, but I can't support no more babies. I just can't, you know. My check look like shit as it is—"

"They garnishing your check?"

"Nah, man. But I gives to my kids. I'm a man—I do the right thing."

That's what you supposed to do. Donovan picked up the napkin and wiped his mouth.

"Uh-huh."

"So she was all like, I'm gonna have this baby whether you gonna be around or not. I said fine, but that's your decision and I can't make you do nothing you don't want to do. So see ya, have a nice life."

"Word?"

"Yeah, man, she wanna be unreasonable, let her."

"How long ago was that?"

"'Bout a month now."

"She get it done?"

"What?"

"The abortion?"

"Well see, that's where the letter comes in, 'cause I ain't calling her or nothing. I see her number on my caller ID, I don't pick up. I done changed my cell phone number and all that. Dig it—I don't even answer my bell when it rings. If I ain't expecting you, then you ain't getting in, ya know."

"Yeah."

"So I gets this letter a few days ago talking about how much she love me and why I'm treating her like this and all this kind of bullshit. But the clincher is this—"

"Yeah?"

"She said if I don't respond to the letter, she gonna kill herself."

"Word?"

Shit, Donovan thinks.

"Yeah, man. Now tell me, do it even sound like I wanna have a crazy bitch like that having my baby?"

"Nah, man. Did you respond?"

"Hell no!"

"You think she gonna do it?"

"Hell no."

You never know.

Donovan pushes the plate away from him and props his elbows up on the bar.

The men talked some more before finally draining their glasses and disappearing out through the door. They'd nodded at Donovan, and the one with the crazy woman had even wished him well. "Have a good night, my brother," he'd said.

Donovan drained the last bit of beer from his bottle and snatched up the napkin to wipe his mouth.

"You want another, Don?"

Nadine, the bartender, leaned over the bar and batted her eyes at him. She had on a black T-shirt that was cut in a long *V* at the front, giving Donovan full view of her cleavage. She smiled and licked her champagne-colored lips.

Donovan smiled back and shook his head. "Anything else I can get for you, then?" Nadine purred.

Donovan shook his head again and tried to keep his smile at a minimum. She was cute and sexy, and if Donovan wanted her, he supposed he could have her, but he had seen her play this same game with him and a dozen other men who came into the bar. He hadn't pursued her, but he was sure the others had, and looking at Nadine, he knew she had turned very few of them down.

That's not the type of woman he wanted.

"How much?" Donovan said, reaching into his back pocket for his wallet.

"Free, if you give me your number," Nadine said as she cleared the plate and glass away.

"Okay, then. So this twenty should cover everything and," Donovan ripped another five from the wallet and set it down on top of the twenty. "And this is for you," he said.

She slid the five-dollar bill across the bar, rolled it between her fingers until it was cigarette thin, and then slipped it down between her breasts. "Thank you." The words oozed from her mouth, and Donovan remembered just how long it had been since he'd had sex.

"Night, Nadine," he said as he walked out the door.

"Bye, Don," she replied, and blew him a kiss.

By the time he warmed up his Daytona and tuned the radio to WBLS, the "quiet storm" was in full swing, and he knew he would have love songs all the way home. He pulled out and onto Fulton Street. There were green lights all ahead of him, and so he moved into fourth and pressed his foot down on the gas until the speedometer danced on fifty.

He'd be home in less than ten minutes if he made all the lights. He had worked overtime that day, and fatigue was slowly creeping through him.

He put a little more weight on the gas pedal.

Tomorrow was another day, and he had put his name down on the overtime list. His boss would call him in the morning if they needed him. They always needed him.

He glanced down at the dashboard. Sixty miles per hour now.

The lights were jumping to yellow with each intersection he took.

He felt he could make at least two more.

Sixty-five.

The snow whipped around his car as the wind picked up. He turned on the wipers. The light turned red as he approached Utica Avenue, but he couldn't stop, he was going too fast and so he held his breath, glanced in the rearview mirror, and shot across the intersection.

The light ahead was red, and he geared down from fourth to second; the tires spun and then gripped just as a woman bolted out in front of him. She never even looked at him, but he imagined her eyes must have been as wide as silver dollars—that's usually how they were when you were screaming bloody murder.

They had all taken turns getting their palms read, and now it was Campbell's turn. It seemed like a good idea at the time, a fun thing to do—well, most things seemed entertaining when your blood was swimming with alcohol.

She would kick herself in the morning when she woke with a pounding headache and an empty wallet.

"You worry about your parents, no?" the psychic said.

Campbell just shrugged her shoulders, fingered the penguin pendant that hung from a delicate gold chain around her neck, and looked off toward her group of girlfriends huddled at a nearby table, pointing and laughing.

Campbell crossed her eyes and stuck her tongue out at them.

The woman cleared her throat.

"I guess," Campbell said, straightening her back.

The woman cocked her head to the side. "You don't believe, huh?"

Campbell just shrugged her shoulders.

"Your parents, they will be fine." The woman pulled Campbell's hand close to her face. "Hmmmmm," she sounded, and Campbell pinched her lips together to keep from smiling.

"You have a question. Ask it," the woman said without looking up.

Campbell hadn't sat down with a question in mind. Was a question like a wish? Did she get three? Would they come true? She had to pick carefully, then. A giggle escaped her, and she moved her free hand to cover her mouth.

The woman raised her eyes, and a slow smile took over her lips. "You are lonely, yes? You want to know when you will meet your soul mate."

Campbell twisted in her chair. "Well—," she started but the woman cut her off.

"You have been alone for a while. Someone—" The woman's eyes went narrow, and she shook her head. "Andre?" she said, and waited for Campbell to react, but Campbell kept a straight face, even though the liquor seemed to be draining from her body, even though her heart was thumping loudly in her chest. "Andre, he hurt you even though you act as if he didn't."

Campbell was sober now. She looked over at her friends again. Had they set this up? How did this woman know about Andre?

Campbell started to feel angry.

"You have a question. Ask it," the woman said again, and waited.

Campbell wanted her hand back, wanted to get up and slap each and every one of those smiling faces she had thought were her friends. What kind of cheap trick were they trying to run on her?

It wasn't funny, not at all.

She looked at the woman and scowled.

"There is someone coming. He will be loving and looking for love, not like your last lover."

Campbell smirked.

"I see the name Mark," she said, and her dark eyes bore into Campbell's. "Do you know a Mark?"

Campbell did, but not any that fit that description, not any that she would be interested in. "No," she lied.

"Hmmmm, this man has very tired feet—he has been walking through your life for many years."

Campbell said nothing.

"The two of you have been together in a former life."

Campbell rolled her eyes.

"You will meet again at a gathering." The woman stopped, bit her lip, and looked a bit more intensely into Campbell's palm. "Not a wedding, but . . . ," she trailed off. "I see a full moon. Music."

Campbell really wanted her hand back.

The woman, sensing Campbell's uneasiness and skepticism, released her hand.

"Twenty dollars," she announced, and presented Campbell with her own open palm.

Campbell hated to admit it, but she had spent most of that spring and the better part of the summer waiting for that man to turn up.

But by the time August rolled in with its stifling heat, the geraniums in the flower boxes were wilted and the young girls and boys who had spent the summer on the streets and odd days at the city pool were toasted golden brown, and Levina Jackson, her next-door neighbor, was ringing the bell and knocking on the door and even leaning over the railing and tapping the tip of her house key on the front window.

Campbell thought that maybe there was a fire somewhere close or that one of Levina's four children was sick.

It had to be one or all of those things because the tapping, knocking, and ringing all screamed, *Urgent.*

Campbell swung the door open, and the tiny bit of cool the house had managed to hold on to escaped, and Levina smiled at her and said good afternoon and asked about Macon and mentioned the heat and the lack of rain and a number of other things that Campbell could not care less about.

Campbell just stared at her.

Levina, with her tattered black head rag and yellow tube top that did nothing for those double-D-cup breasts she had. It took a good ten minutes for Levina to deliver some neighborhood gossip, say hello to Old Man Sumner, who was more than happy to stop and tell her how fine she looked in yellow. "Yes, indeed— yes, indeed," he said, never once looking at her face.

"Mailman put this in my mailbox," she said when Campbell felt she couldn't look interested in what Levina was saying a moment longer.

Levina pulled an envelope from the back pocket of those cut-off overwashed denim shorts she'd donned every Saturday since June.

"Thanks," Campbell said, and closed the door on Levina and the heat.

The envelope was folded in two and wilted, like Levina had had the envelope tucked away against her behind for a week.

She didn't notice the return address, just her name, and she ripped the flap open and pulled out the fine vanilla-colored stationery.

She read the letter four times and still didn't quite understand what was happening.

A woman, Dottie McPherson of McPherson Artist Representatives, had loved the Polaroids of her five collages and had a special fondness for the one titled *Sweet Thang*, and wondered how many more she had and would she mind showing all of them to her.

She'd shared the Polaroids with a gallery owner in the Village, and he'd been just as excited about her work, and now they both thought she was an undiscovered talent.

Dottie wrote that she would love to represent her and was sure that she would have a gallery showing arranged before the ink had dried on the dotted line of their contract.

She thought the pieces were *phenomenal* (a word she used relentlessly throughout the letter) and would Campbell please call her as soon as possible at any of the three numbers listed below?

Campbell looked at the front of the envelope. It was her name and address typed neatly across it, but why did what was happening feel like it belonged to someone else?

She hadn't sent out any Polaroids, not one.

Had considered it, but had never done it. She had collages all over the place, framed on the walls, stacked away in the basement. Making collages had been her salvation, the distraction Dr. Bing had suggested she find, her therapy.

Campbell looked at the envelope again.

Could Macon have sent them off? Why would she do something like that without discussing it with her first?

Because you would have said no; you always say no. Always too afraid to take a chance on yourself.

Her subconscious was right. She was afraid to take a chance on herself, her happiness.

Are you happy now?

Sure, I'm happy for Macon, proud, too—

(But are you happy for yourself?)

Was she?

Not really.

She was thirty-four years old and still biting her tongue at the American Airlines ticket counters. Sure, she'd been an employee long enough to have weekends and holidays off.

Yes, she'd been practically around the world. But when she and Pat took the kids to the park and spent the day walking, laughing, and talking about where their lives would be in ten or more years, she never thought she'd still be greeting polite, irate, and indifferent airline passengers with, "Good morning. How can I help you today?"

She supposed she wasn't really happy. No one in that house had been for a long time. Not the tenant, Clarence, who referred to himself as an old queen now. He'd had numerous lovers since Awed left. But now he was alone and spent the warm summer weekends seated in the front yard in his green-and-white folding chair, sipping Sprite and watching the world go by.

Millie hadn't been happy either, but Campbell suspected her unhappiness had started long before they moved to Bainbridge Street, although after Campbell had had the baby, there seemed to be some sort of reprieve to her misery.

Macon had brought some joy into that house; she'd been happy from birth.

When they laid Macon on her chest, pink, wiggling, and wet, the first thought that came to Campbell's fifteen-year-old mind was that John Carpenter movie, *The Thing*.

Well, her mind was still twisted from the contractions, still pounding from the doctors, nurses, and Millie telling her to breathe and not to push and then to push. They wouldn't let Luscious in, so she spent the whole time outside the delivery room pacing and cussing at the front desk nurses.

"Okay, push," the doctor said somewhere down at her feet. Her knees were up and her legs apart, and the doctor was crouched down on a stool at the foot of the bed, white mask stretched across his face, white knit cap pulled down over his blond curls. Campbell thought he looked like an umpire. "Push, Campbell, push."

Where was the baseball mitt?

She was delirious.

"Baby, please push," Millie said, her eyes all puffed and red from lack of sleep and the sobbing she fell into whenever Campbell cried out in pain.

Campbell couldn't push, as much as she wanted it out and the pain over; the only strength she had left in her she used for screaming.

"Push!" the doctor demanded firmly.

Campbell just screamed.

"Goddamnit," the doctor muttered, and in one frustrated move he jumped up and snatched his mask off his face. "The baby is right there, right there. One push, please," he pleaded.

Campbell screamed again.

"Oh, Lord God have mercy!" Luscious howled from the hallway.

Millie's bottom lip trembled, and she felt a set of fresh tears coming on. "Please, Campbell, please," she coaxed, and grabbed Campbell's hand. "Just try."

It hurt in every place on her body. Her stomach, back, down between her legs, the tips of her toes, and who knew that the hair on her head had sensation, because that hurt, too.

But she finally let loose, squeezed her eyes shut, and pushed with all her might, and six pounds three ounces of baby girl came shooting out of her, taking the doctor completely off guard. He would have missed, and she would have landed on the floor, but at the very last second he caught her by her ankles.

Luscious couldn't take it anymore, she'd been pacing that hall for what seemed like hours, and she'd counted on her fingers the number of times Campbell had cried out, and when she ran out of fingers she started counting her toes—and now she was counting the tiny lines that represented the seconds on the large black clock on the wall and was down to the last line when Campbell's scream tore through her.

She stormed past the nurses' station and knocked the heavyset male orderly aside with one blow and burst through the doors cussing and accusing the doctors of allowing Campbell to remain in pain for so long just because she was black.

"White folks get shots and pills, all kinds of things to dull the pain. Ain't we suffered enough? Guess not, four hundred years of slavery wasn't enough, was it?"

Security was on their way down to remove Luscious from the delivery room and the building by the time Millie started screaming, "Rita, calm down, please."

There was a chorus going on in that room, everyone shouting and yelling, Luscious lunging at the doctor, one small Puerto Rican nurse crouching in the corner with a scalpel in her hand for protection, while the other nurse stood in the middle of all the mayhem, waving her arms.

Campbell, calm now, looked down into her daughter's newborn face, and seeing that child, barely three minutes old, eyes wide open and laughing, everything else dropped away.

Campbell smiled at the memory.

Perhaps it was time for her to be happy, too; her daughter evidently thought so.

She went upstairs and picked up the phone.

Solomon had retired from the post office and had taken a part-time security job at Brooklyn Hospital, working a rotating shift that kept him out of the house four out of seven days.

He had all but stopped talking about Daisy, and since Donovan had moved into the upstairs apartment and gotten his own number, Solomon didn't have to hear Daisy's voice on the other end asking to speak to Donovan.

The top apartment was a spacious two bedroom that was in great need of repair. The paint was old and peeling, the kitchen was outdated, and there was mold growing on the walls and ceiling. Around the mouth of the fireplace, whole blocks of ceramic tile were either missing, cracked, or discolored, and the hardwood floors were warped and bulging.

"Sure does need a lot of work," Solomon had said as he stepped around boxes of clothing and whatnots that Grammy had left up there years ago.

Donovan folded his arms and looked around him. "Well, Dad, that's the beauty of it," he said.

Donovan had no problem immersing himself in work. Work kept his mind off everything else in life.

A plate of whatever Grammy had cooked that night, maybe a beer, and more often than not he would be dozing in front of the television before nine o'clock.

There were few women in his life: Grammy, Daisy, Elaine, some female cousins, women whom he'd known since high school, wives of his friends.

No romantic entanglements for him. Not for the moment, anyway.

Women, he thought, always seemed to want too much.

Too much time, too much money. They looked at his car, his clothing, and the gold watch he wore around his wrist and started making assumptions. "No children?" "Never been married?" "A motorman? They make damn good money, don't they?"

He was a "fine catch," Grammy said. "Be careful—women can be barracudas. They'll suck you in and spit you out, and you won't even know it until you're a wad of gunk on the bottom of their shoe," she said.

"All women aren't like that," his sister Elaine would laugh when he shared Grammys philosophies with her. "Some women just want a man for who he is, not what he has."

Donovan supposed it was true. But he had been burned twice. Once with Laura and the other time with Nina.

He'd loved both of them, had bent every rule he and Grammy had created for himself, but in the end, he'd found himself alone.

"Well, I have yet to meet her," Donovan said, and lifted his two-month-old nephew from the crib.

He wanted children, he knew that. Elaine had three, and he spent as much time with them as he could.

Elaine sighed as she watched her brother gently cradle her son. "You know you need a woman to make a child."

Donovan smirked—he knew. He knew.

Campbell hadn't been in a real relationship for over two years when she decided to sit in the seat next to Elaine, and said hello.

It was a poetry class, something she had always been interested in and now had the time to pursue. Once a week, Wednesdays, from seven until nine, reading and reciting and picking apart Langston, Nikki, and Amiri.

They'd gotten to know each other in bits and pieces during the elevator rides and the fifteen-minute breaks spent huddled around the coffee machine in the cafeteria.

Sometimes they even walked out together. Elaine's husband, Larry, smiling at her from the front seat of their Jeep, the three kids bundled up and sleeping in the back.

Campbell took the train.

They hadn't exchanged numbers, the relationship hadn't

grown beyond school, but Campbell felt comfortable enough to slip her an invitation to her art show.

"Oh, my God!" Elaine squealed.

Campbell just smiled. "It's no big deal, really. Just you know, fifteen collages."

"I've been sitting next to a celebrity all this time!" Elaine laughed, and slapped playfully at Campbell's arm.

"Oh, please." Campbell blushed and waved the comment away. "If you can't make it, I understand. Maybe you can just pass it on to someone who might be interested."

"Of course I'll be there. Wow. Are you going to tell the professor?"

"Well, yes, I think so, but you know I don't want to make a big deal out of it."

"It *is* a big deal, Campbell."

"Thanks."

"You know." Elaine stepped closer to Campbell, and her eyes took on a mischievous look. "If it's okay, I'd like to bring my brother along."

"Okay." Campbell shrugged her shoulders.

"I mean bring him so you two could meet, you know?"

Campbell wasn't sure about that.

"He's single, no children, and doing okay for himself. He works for transit, a motorman. Maybe you two should get together—you're not married, right? Just you and your daughter? I think he might like your smile."

Campbell blushed.

Earlier that day the air had been damp and the sky gray. The weather report called for rain, but none ever came and the seagulls that did not normally stray from the swampy areas of land that surrounded Kennedy Airport were spotted searching for worms along the side streets off Flatbush Avenue.

But by five o'clock the clouds had evaporated and the sky was dark blue, stars strewn here and there with a cumbersome yellow moon situated at its center.

Simone's Art Gallery sat at the base of a six-story apartment building situated at the corner of Saint Marks Avenue and Flatbush. It was a cozy space with two overstuffed couches and old mahogany bookshelves the owner had rescued from a library upstate.

The walls were painted a stark white, which seemed to make the colorful collages jump out at you.

The turnout was small. The majority of the people who came were friends and family. The owner, Simone Nicole, a white woman with a long reddish-gray mane that seemed to be more than her four-foot-two stature could handle, had walked over to Campbell and squeezed her elbow excitedly. "Mr. Henry Parsons has just bought five of your pieces!"

Campbell didn't know who Henry Parsons was. "Which five?" Campbell had asked as she scanned the room to find the buyer.

Simone had stumbled backwards a bit as her face registered disbelief. "Henry Parsons is a very wealthy art enthusiast. He owns a collection worth millions."

Campbell nodded. "Oh."

Simone placed her hands on her head, and her tiny fingers disappeared. "Campbell," Simone's voice became shrill. "You have just made yourself sixty thousand dollars!"

It was Campbell's turn to take a step backwards.

"Well, before my thirty percent and your agent's twenty." Simone added quickly. "And Campbell, it's just opening night!" Simone stepped forward and gave Campbell a hearty hug.

Campbell couldn't recall too much of what went on after she'd received that news from Simone. She did remember kissing her mother and daughter good-bye. Walking some former coworkers to the door, Anita's perfume, the way Laverna's arm draped around the waist of her mate, the aquamarine turtleneck Porsche wore, and the bewitching music that seeped from the apartment above, somehow making her miss Pat more than ever.

They were late, and Campbell already had her coat in her hand; she was saying good-bye to some people, and the lights at the back of the gallery were already turned off.

Her eyes caught Elaine's first and then his. She gave them a little three-finger wave and mouthed hello before turning her attention back to Simone's husband, a light-skinned man with a bald head who barely reached Campbell's shoulder. She had to stoop down a little when he threw his arm over her shoulder and whispered something in her ear, before kissing her on the cheek.

It was a lingering kiss that for some reason made Donovan feel uncomfortable. He found himself staring, and when Campbell's eyes found him again, he quickly looked down at his watch.

"Oh," Elaine cried. "I'm sorry we're so late," she said when Campbell approached them. "Donovan worked late today and didn't get home until forty minutes ago," she said, and threw Donovan an annoyed look.

"Yeah, it was my fault," Donovan said, and stuck his hand out to Campbell. "Look at that, we've just met and already I'm apologizing," he said, and grinned.

"Oh, it's okay." Campbell wrapped her hand in his and smiled.

Later on in life Campbell would wonder about that moment and marvel at how clearly she'd been able to see through the wall he'd erected around himself.

He was tall and just a shade or two darker than Campbell. Not really her type—she usually went for darker men. But his eyes were nice, round and clear, long lashes with dark bushy eyebrows.

"Did you have a lot of people?" Elaine asked.

"Just about twenty. That's all."

"Where are your parents, your daughter?"

"They went on home."

"Did you make any sales?"

"Uhm, five." Campbell beamed.

"Go ahead, girl!" Elaine squealed.

Donovan looked around at the collages, his eyes focused on the white tabs situated below the artwork that gave the title of the piece and the price.

He made a sound and tried to disguise it as a cough. He sure wasn't about to whip out his American Express card and charge seven grand for a piece of paper with pictures plastered all over it. No way.

Elaine looked at her watch. "Can I at least look around? I might see something, and you can go home and tell everybody you sold six pieces instead of five." Elaine strolled off to the right, beginning at the *Sweet Thang* collage. Donovan followed close behind.

Campbell had a thing about the way men walked. She sized them up and tore them down based on their stride. Now, standing there, watching Donovan walk straight-backed with head slightly tilted toward the sky, she was reminded of the proud Masai tribesmen she'd seen on the pages of *National Geographic* and then again in real life on the sandy shores of Diani Beach in Kenya.

"These are beautiful." Elaine's voice shattered Campbell's thoughts.

"Thank you."

"What do you think, Donovan?" Campbell asked.

She wanted to look at him again, see him from the front; she'd missed the ample lips and meticulously groomed mustache. Were those dimples hollowed into his cheeks?

Donovan was standing at Elaine's shoulder, staring at a piece titled *Crime and Punishment*; he turned to address Campbell. "I don't know a whole lot about art, but this is kinda cool," he said, pointing to the collage.

"Thanks." Campbell was a bit embarrassed. The *Crime and Punishment* collage depicted violence and death; it was put together during one of her very dark periods.

"These are simply wonderful, Campbell," Elaine said, her voice filled with awe. "I have to say that one of your collages is simply not in my budget this month." Elaine gave a little laugh.

"Well, maybe next month, then," Campbell said, and winked at her as Simone handed her her coat.

"More like next year," Elaine said, still laughing as she started toward the door.

"So," Campbell said as they huddled together in front of the gallery. "Where to now?"

"Well, Donovan is going to drop me back at the house, and you two are going to get something to eat."

Campbell wasn't sure she was ready to be left alone with him. Blind dates are always so awkward.

"You're not going to eat with us?" Campbell hoped her voice didn't sound too desperate.

"Nope. I've got to get back home to the kids." She winked at them and grinned.

Donovan walked ahead of the women. He didn't know why he'd allowed his sister to talk him into this. She was always trying to fix him up with someone. He was perfectly happy being alone. Well, at least most of the time.

He looked at his watch again. It was nine o'clock, he'd

worked all day and had had only about five hours' sleep, and he was already yawning. This woman was going to think he was boring. Why the hell did he agree to this?

He snatched a look over his shoulder at Campbell. She was cute, he thought, and yes, he did like her smile.

He stopped alongside a black two-door Mercedes coupe, his newest possession—he'd had it for only a few months, and the inside still carried that just-off-the-assembly-line new car smell.

Donovan opened the passenger door and folded the seat forward.

Well, it was her brother's car, Campbell thought to herself, and started to climb into the back. Elaine caught her by the shoulder. "No, no. You're the guest. I'll sit in the back," she said, and hopped in.

To Campbell's relief Elaine talked nonstop for the whole ten minutes they were in the car together. When they turned onto Saint Felix Street, Campbell let out a small giggle of surprise.

"What?" Donovan asked as he slowed the car to a stop.

"My mother used to have a friend who lived over here," she said, and pressed her index finger into her chin. "I think it was that house, the white one with the awning over the doorway." She spoke slowly as she forced herself to remember.

"Really?" Elaine said as she squinted at the house. "Does she still live there?"

"No, she moved about twelve or so years ago. She gave the best barbecues."

"Was her name Pullman?" Donovan asked as he stepped out of the car and folded his seat forward.

"Uh-huh, Loretta Pullman, I think," Campbell said.

"Yeah, I remember her."

"Wow, six degrees of separation, huh?" Elaine said as she climbed out of the car.

"What?" Donovan gave her a quizzical look.

"You know, the theory that there are only six people between you and someone you don't know," she said, and then bent down and looked at Campbell. "You and Donovan probably saw one another when you were kids. I guess you were just destined to meet."

Campbell just smiled and shrugged her shoulders. "I guess," she said.

Elaine bade them good night. Kissed Donovan on the cheek and winked at Campbell. "Y'all have a good time."

"So where would you like to eat?" he said as he shot a quick glance at the dashboard clock. It was nine-twenty. He stifled a yawn and turned onto Fulton Street.

"Uhm, well, anyplace is good."

She realized she was sitting at attention, knees pressed together, hands folded tightly in her lap. She tried to convince herself to relax, to allow her eyes to enjoy the scenery, her mind to concentrate on the soft music streaming from the radio, but all she could think of was if she'd put on enough deodorant and if she'd been successful at brushing away the salmon she'd had for lunch.

She hated blind dates.

"Well, have you ever been to Baxter's?" he asked, and then shifted into a higher gear, pulling past a van.

"Yes, once," Campbell said as her left hand gripped the soft leather of the armrest.

Donovan caught the move. "Are you nervous?" He laughed and shifted down from fourth to third gear.

"No," Campbell lied.

"Don't worry; I know what I'm doing. You've got a lot of assholes out here who don't. Me, I drive every day. Most of these clowns out here only drive on the weekends, you know?"

Campbell nodded her head and released the armrest.

"Do you drive?" he asked as he slowed up to take a corner.

"Well, I don't own a car or anything, but I do have my license. I rent cars when I need to—and that's not often. I really don't need a car. . . . I really don't like driving anyway. . . ." The words spilled from her mouth like floodwaters. She knew she was babbling but couldn't get herself to stop.

Donovan nodded and remarked when needed until Campbell finally ended her litany with, "Yes, yes, I do drive." She blushed at her foolishness. "I guess that was the long answer."

Donovan nodded his head in agreement and stopped near a narrow space between two cars. "You think I can fit in there?" he said, already undoing his seat belt and putting the car in reverse.

Campbell turned her head to look at the space. It looked too small to her, but then again, she wasn't good at parking. "I don't know," she uttered in an unsure voice.

Donovan threw his arm around the back of Campbell's seat and leaned toward her a bit as he stared out the back window and approximated the space he had. She could smell his cologne and see the small lightning bolt scar on his left cheek, above the dimple.

She was staring at him. He could feel her eyes on his face like fingers, and as much as he wanted to look down at her, he didn't, he just concentrated on the space between his bumper and the one attached to the Honda behind him that had a blaring sticker that said DENTISTS DO IT WITH FLOSS.

Baxter's was packed.

A jazz band played loud and furiously close to the front entrance, and all the tables were filled with the Fort Greene residents who were more than happy to be able to drink, dance, and socialize just steps away from their homes and apartments.

The Fort Greene, Park Slope, and Clinton Hill neighborhoods had all undergone extensive renovations over the past few years. Neighborhoods that once housed burnt-out buildings and crack-littered sidewalks were now buppie and yuppie meccas.

High-end shops and restaurants dotted Fulton Street and Dekalb Avenue, and white people, once a rarity in those neighborhoods, were now more than forty percent of the population.

He hadn't opened the car door for her. Well, she hadn't given him a chance. She was up and out of the car before Donovan had even put the car in park good.

She wanted desperately to be out and away from that small space.

Donovan jumped in front of Campbell just as her hand was about to catch hold of the restaurant's doorknob. "Can you let me be a gentleman?" he said, his voice full of amusement as he yanked the door open.

"Certainly," Campbell retorted before she stepped over the threshold.

"I don't think we're going to get a table," Campbell screamed over the music.

"Yeah, we will—there are more tables in the back," Donovan said, and pressed his hand firmly into the small of her back to guide her. "You're not going to be mobbed by dozens of adoring fans, are you?" he bent over, and whispered to her.

When was the last time a man whispered in her ear? She couldn't remember. "Oh please," Campbell laughed. "Nobody knows me."

"I do," he said, and Campbell could have sworn his eyes sparkled.

"Two," Donovan mouthed, and held up two fingers.

The woman, a large busty Latina, smiled warmly at him. "Sure, Don," she said before giving Campbell a quick once-over and turning to indicate that they should follow her.

Campbell made a face at her back.

She seated them in a dark corner adjacent to two other couples who were too engrossed in their meals and conversation to pay them any mind.

Donovan pulled Campbell's chair out for her.

That was nice, she thought to herself. Chivalry was something she appreciated; she checked off one point for Donovan.

Campbell ordered a glass of white wine, and Donovan, a Heineken.

"So, how long have you been making collages?" he said after they'd placed their dinner orders.

"Oh, on and off for the past few years."

"Elaine tells me you used to work for the airlines?"

"Yep."

"Flight attendant?"

"Ticket agent."

"Oh."

There was a quiet moment when both of them allowed their eyes to survey their surroundings. Donovan called for another beer and without asking ordered another glass of wine for Campbell.

"That's, uhm, cute," Donovan said suddenly, pointing at the pendant.

Campbell's fingers went immediately to the pendant. "Oh, thanks," she said as her index finger stroked the metal.

Donovan leaned his head in and squinted. "What is it?"

Campbell leaned away from him. "A penguin."

"Huh," Donovan sounded, and leaned back into his chair. "You like penguins, do you?" he remarked before tilting his bottle to his lips.

Campbell just shrugged her shoulders. "They're okay, I guess," she lied. Campbell had been collecting penguins since she and Andre had split. Collecting them and hoping that they would somehow influence her love life.

There was another lengthy silence as Campbell fingered the pendant and tried hard not to look at Donovan.

"So you have children?" Donovan finally broke the silence.

"One. A girl. Eighteen."

Donovan's eyes went wide. "Eighteen? Well, how old are you?"

She still got defensive when people reacted that way to the fact that she had a grown child. She remembered the women, women her mother's age, looking at her with disgust, pity, or both whenever they happened upon her pushing Macon in her stroller.

"You know you don't ask a woman's age." Campbell tried to make her voice sound light.

"Sorry, I guess her age just took me off guard."

"You're apologizing to me again," Campbell joked before taking a sip of her wine.

"I am, aren't I?" he laughed, and shook his head.

"Well, I'm thirty-four," She said.

Campbell could see Donovan doing the math in his head. "Wow, you were really young."

"Yeah, I was." Campbell bit her bottom lip and looked around the room.

Donovan watched her thoughtfully for a moment. "Well, I don't have any. Kids, that is."

Good, the spotlight was off her for the moment. "How come?"

It was a stupid question, and she wanted to kick herself for asking, but she hadn't come across a lot of men in their mid-thirties who hadn't had at least one child.

Maybe he can't have any. Maybe he's sterile, did you ever think of that? her mind chastised her.

"Good condoms, I guess." His response was so matter-of-fact, his face so serious when he said it that it was comical, and Campbell burst out laughing.

The tension and uneasiness slipped away after that, and they were able to converse on a more comfortable level.

Their conversation tottered on to his job and her new career, places she'd been and the ones he hoped to visit one day, her parents and his. Music, sports, and everything else in between.

They were studying the dessert menu when Donovan looked at Campbell, folded his hands, and asked, "So why aren't you married?" The question was so abrupt that for a minute Campbell thought she hadn't heard right.

"Oh, uhm." She snatched a quick look at his eyes before looking back down at her menu. "I guess I just haven't found the right person yet."

Again his question rekindled that defensive feeling that had crept through her earlier in the evening. Her eyes moved between the crème brûlée and apple tart as her mind tried to ignore the questions she had often asked herself over the years.

Is something wrong with me? Am I not pretty enough, thin enough? Are my breasts too small, ass too big? Teeth not white enough, skin too dark, too light? Is it me, is it me, is it me?

Campbell put the menu down and excused herself to the ladies' room.

Donovan stood up when she stood.

That's what a gentleman does, although it wasn't something he often did when he was with a woman. And him doing it now, without even thinking about it, surprised him.

He watched Campbell walk away. He liked her walk. It was an easy and unhurried stride. Sexy, he thought.

He found himself standing and staring long after she'd pushed open the door marked WOMEN and disappeared.

She was well built—*thick* would be the street phrase used to describe her. Wide hips, round behind that rode back. *Juicy* is what came to Donovan's mind.

He'd kept his eyes focused on her face during dinner, the sleepy bedroom eyes and pouty lips. But he'd managed to treat himself to her ample cleavage at the gallery when her attention was focused elsewhere.

In the bathroom, Campbell examined her face in the mirror as she washed her hands.

There were specks of mascara caught on her eyelids, and—surprise, surprise—the lipstick she'd applied just three hours ago was faded away. *Long lasting, my foot,* she thought as she dug her makeup case out of her pocketbook.

She turned Donovan's questions over and over in her mind. They were just questions, she told herself. That's what people do when they're trying to get to know you. Didn't she ask him a few of her own? *Stop being so damn sensitive, he wasn't judging you, just trying to know you.*

She powdered her face and put a new coat of lipstick on her lips. She wanted to take down her hair. Her head was beginning to pound beneath the tension of the rubber band, but then she decided just to deal with it. A glance at her watch told her that they wouldn't be there too much longer anyhow.

He stood up again when she came back. "Hello again," she breathed before sitting down. "So why aren't *you* married?" The question shot out of her, surprising both of them.

Donovan laughed so hard tears came to his eyes. "Damn," he said, and wiped at the corners of his eyes. "I don't know. Same reason as you, I guess."

He was about to say something else when the waitress approached and set two more drinks down on the table.

"We didn't order another round," Donovan said as the waitress cleared away the empty glasses.

"From the gentleman at the bar." She pointed over her shoulder to a brown-skinned man with salt-and-pepper hair. He was smiling at them and holding his glass up in salute.

Both Donovan and Campbell nodded their heads in acceptance and thanks.

"Do you know him?" They asked each other in unison.

A pause.

"No," they announced together.

Campbell looked over at the man again. He did look a bit familiar, but Campbell was having a hard time placing him. The man was still smiling, his head moving between Campbell and the group of people that stood alongside him.

"Oh," a sigh of relief escaping her, "he was at the gallery tonight."

Thank you, she mouthed, and the gentleman saluted her again.

"Well, that was nice of him."

"Yes, very," Campbell agreed, and picked up her fourth glass of wine for the evening.

"You were about to say something before the waitress came over."

Donovan twisted his mouth and rolled his eyes up into his head. "Let's see, hmmm. Oh, yeah, what I was going to say was that I think I'm ready now."

Campbell stared at him.

"You know, ready to get married, settle down, have a few kids?" Based on the look Campbell was giving him, he felt she needed further clarification.

Campbell had never heard a man admit to being ready for a commitment. "Really?" is all she could bring herself to say.

Suddenly, Donovan reached over and grabbed her hand. "Do you want to dance?" he asked, and his face lit up.

"To this?" Campbell laughed, and nodded her head toward the band. "This is not dancing music."

Donovan grinned. "We could go someplace else. Someplace close."

Campbell was really enjoying herself, but she'd had a long day, too. She mentally counted off the number of beers he'd consumed, and felt it was the alcohol talking and not him.

She looked down at her watch. It was close to one. "Can't we do it next time?" she said sweetly.

Donovan looked down at his own watch. "It is kind of late, huh?" A small yawn escaped him. "Remember when one o'clock was early?" He laughed and motioned for the check.

"Yes, I do," Campbell laughed, and rested her chin on her hands. "I must have been twenty-five years old."

The ride home was quiet, but the silence was comfortable now.

"I really had a good time, Donovan. Thanks so much," she said as she clutched her keys in her hand.

"Me, too."

"Well," Campbell started, and reached for the door.

"So when can I see you again?"

The car door was open just a bit, and she pulled it shut again and turned to face him. She wanted to say, Anytime you want. Me, I'm always available. I like you and would love to see you again. Is tomorrow too soon?

But instead she said, "Call me."

"Can I have your number, then, please?"

"Sure."

Donovan leaned over her and opened the glove compartment. He fumbled for a pen and then found a slip of paper—a parking ticket he'd neglected to pay—and for the second time that night Campbell was privy to an up close and personal view.

She thought his hair was wavy, but now on closer inspection, she could see that it was actually a mass of tight curls. His neck was thick and smooth; he had dabbed cologne there, too, because it wafted up and around her and she inhaled it like air.

Donovan wrote his number down first. Home and cell phone.

Wow, Campbell thought to herself, he really didn't want to miss her call. She wrote down her home number and handed it to him.

"Do you have a cell phone?" he asked after scrutinizing the numbers and reciting them to make sure he was reading them correctly.

Campbell nodded.

"Uh-huh, I see. You don't want a brother hunting you down, huh?" he said slyly.

Campbell just grinned. "Well, thanks again." She said, "Have a good night, and drive safely." She stepped out and shut the door.

Donovan waited until she was inside the house and waving before he honked his horn once and drove off.

I wonder if I should have given him a kiss good-bye, Campbell thought to herself as she climbed the stairs to her bedroom.

Damn, Donovan thought as he took the corner, *not even a kiss good night.*

A week passed and then two, and Campbell still hadn't heard from Donovan.

She was sick with herself for checking the caller ID, jumping when the phone rang, and then feeling sorry that it wasn't him when she answered it.

Hadn't they had a good time?

She thought they had.

Wasn't he the one to ask when he could see her again?

Yes, yes, she'd heard right.

Men could be so damn frustrating!

"Well, why don't you call him, Campbell? It's not the 1800s, you know. Women can be assertive—it's acceptable—hell, it's expected!" Laverna had advised when Campbell complained to her.

She'd tried a dozen times to do just that, had picked up the phone and dialed six of the seven numbers and then hung up.

Why should she have to call?

Why not? the voice inside her mind asked.

"Later for him," she said aloud to herself one day when all she could think of was him and that night.

"Jerk," she said as she crumpled the paper that held all his numbers and dropped them in the garbage.

Donovan had been working nonstop.

Double shifts during the week, Saturdays and some Sundays, too. All he could do when he did have a day off was sleep.

Every day he promised himself he'd call Campbell as soon as he got home from work, call while the sun was still up and his mind alert. Every day became tomorrow, and tomorrow stretched into two weeks and then Christmas.

"You still haven't called her?" Elaine screeched from her home in Hempstead.

"I've been busy," Donovan said as he stared into his empty refrigerator for the third time that day. "You want to come over and do some food shopping for me?" he teased.

Elaine let out a long sigh. "No. Busy doing what, working?"

"You know it."

"Donovan, this is why you don't have any woman. Work will always be there. You've got to give yourself a break, enjoy yourself sometimes."

He did. His break came on Sundays when he lounged around

the apartment all day watching satellite television or listening to music.

"What are you doing with all that money you're making? You're not enjoying it."

"Yes, I am, I have a good ol' time looking at my bank statements." Donovan laughed.

Another sigh. "You know, you're making me look like an idiot. I told her all these great things about you. My brother this and my brother that. You're making me look like a liar. If you didn't like her, then I understand. But you said you had a great time and wouldn't mind seeing her again."

"Has she called you?" Donovan questioned Elaine.

"No, we never exchanged numbers."

"Oh."

"Call her, Donovan!"

"Okay! Damn, Elaine, is she paying you?"

"Call her today, Donovan, today."

"Okay, damn."

January

Like every New Year's Eve before that, Donovan found himself surrounded by family, a little less than sober, wearing a colorful, pointed paper hat, his lips moving from plastic horn to Hennessy-filled plastic cup in short intervals, his ears filled with the sound of music, conversation, and laughter.

Paper plates heavy with chitterlings, black-eyed peas, and collard greens littering everything with a flat surface. Not a dirty piece of clothing in the house and the seventy-eight of "Auld Lang Syne" ready and waiting on the record player.

Everything had been done just so, in order to secure good luck, health, and fortune in the New Year.

He wondered as he wandered through the crowd of relatives if this would be the year that the dreams would stop and the voice would die.

Would this be the year the fear and uneasiness that had settled itself on him like a second skin was finally shed?

He was a grown man, but he still got the sweats and shakes whenever he had to go down into that basement.

The chair was still there and the small table next to it. The twin bedframe, skeletal without the mattress, had been propped upright against the wall.

Donovan would stand there, trying to catch his breath and keep the sweat out of his eyes, but his hands would shake and his lips tremble, and he had to fight with everything in him to keep from running back up the stairs.

He talked to himself while he searched for whatever it was Grammy needed from downstairs. He needed to hear the sound of his own voice, because without it, Clyde's whispers would fill his ears.

"Ain't you got no woman yet?" "When you gonna get married and make some babies, man!" "You ain't getting any younger."

His relatives pelted their questions and smart-ass comments at him like stones.

That was the other problem with these gatherings. He wondered if that problem might be attached to the first, but wasn't sure about that and couldn't bring himself to find out from a professional, a psychologist, because that might mean he was crazy or something worse, and maybe the doctor might want to prescribe pills or electric shock or hypnosis to unearth this thing that had him terrified of the basement, this thing that didn't allow him to trust or to love.

That's what Delia had told him. She'd screamed, "You don't love me completely!"

Donovan pretended not to understand what she meant, but he knew. Three years earlier, Sandra had accused him of not fully loving her.

Nina had never had that complaint. Donovan had relinquished

himself to her, and the wall that he lived behind had crumbled the first day he'd laid eyes on her.

He'd truly thought that she was the one.

Long, leggy, and copper colored, Nina was a wet dream in high heels.

He'd said hello to her one day as she passed by him on the sidewalk. He hadn't expected a response; a woman who looked like that wouldn't give him a second thought. But he'd spoken to her anyway, just because.

He had the wind on his side that day; a sudden October gust caught hold of her hair and lifted the back of her skirt. She giggled, grabbing her long black tresses with one hand and the hem of her skirt with the other, losing hold of the hot dog she'd been carrying, and so it ended down at her feet.

"Can I replace that for you?" he said before he'd even realized he'd formed a question in his mind.

There was no answer from her, just a smile and a nod of her head.

She was intoxicating from the beginning, had him doing things he'd never thought he'd do, kissing her in places he swore he'd never kiss. Giving her money whether she asked for it or not, buying gifts and sending flowers.

Meeting her after work and sometimes for lunch and playing taxi when she went out with her friends and needed a ride.

Buying her a cell phone and paying off those three little credit card bills that were preventing her from getting that new Jeep she wanted, the one he cosigned for.

Grammy would have called him a fool, a goddamn fool, if she knew. She would have said that that woman had put something on him.

Looking back, Donovan would have believed just that. She

must have put something on him, some type of mojo, maybe in his food or down between her legs.

There had to be something, because that other side of him—that bruised and broken part of him that Clyde had left behind, the piece of himself that stopped believing in Santa Claus, the tooth fairy, and happy endings, that little-boy bit of himself that trusted no one—didn't even warn him.

He'd circled the block twice to be sure. There were plenty of black Cherokee Jeeps, but only one with fuchsia-colored iridescent letters across the back windshield that spelled JOY.

It was a quarter to two in the morning, and the traffic that moved up and down Atlantic Avenue was sparse.

Donovan was on his way back from Hempstead, a Saturday-night dinner with his sister and her husband that had led to four games of blackjack and then a ten-minute conversation in the driveway.

He slowed his car down when he saw the vehicle sitting half on and half off the sidewalk beneath the overpass. Came to a complete stop when he was close enough to read the letters in the back window. He cut the lights, as was his habit when he turned off the ignition and exited his car.

The vehicle had to have been stolen. Snatched for a joyride and then dumped there, he told himself.

He crept up along the passenger side of the car.

He'd spoken to Nina at eight, thought that maybe he would drop by after dinner, drop by for some dessert, he'd said.

"I'm having the girls over. I'll see you tomorrow." She'd kissed the receiver three times before hanging up.

Nina was home, sipping wine, playing music, and laughing with her girlfriends; that's why she didn't hear the car alarm, he reasoned.

He pressed his face against the tinted glass window. The keys were dangling from the ignition, and the radio was on.

That's strange, he laughed to himself as he grabbed hold of the door handle.

Nina loved a slow fuck. "Fuck me slow and deep," she'd whisper in his ear when they made love. It made his blood boil just to hear her say it.

"Harder, deeper," she'd demand and claw his back with her fingernails.

Sometimes she'd be on top, touching herself for him, running her tongue across her lips and tilting her head so far back on her neck that he could feel the featherlike ends of her hair brushing against his thighs.

And there she was now, in the same position she'd taken on top of him, making the same demands of someone else.

He'd probably been watching them for a good thirty seconds before the man Nina was on top of opened his eyes and looked dead into Donovan's face.

"Fuck off!" he'd yelled, and the sudden blast of his voice snapped Nina out of her trance, and now Donovan had two sets of eyes glaring at him.

Donovan calmly closed the door and walked back to his car.

For a moment, while the car was still in park, his foot drumming the gas pedal, Clyde was laughing in his head and screeching, *Do it, Cappy. Do it!*

The engine revving, revving—he wanted to do it, wanted to slam into the back of that Cherokee, that JOY vehicle, but that would be cutting his nose off to spite his face, and besides, he thought as he threw the car into drive and sped off, Nina was still on top of him, and the impact might actually give Nina a thrill.

He never asked Nina why. Just went on ahead and had the

Jeep repossessed, changed his telephone number. He had Grammy play gatekeeper when Nina came to the house wanting to explain, needing to talk.

"If you come here again, I'll call the cops on you," Grammy warned her.

He didn't tell anyone what had happened, but Grammy knew that whatever it was it had to be bad, because she hadn't seen her grandson's eyes look that vacant since that steamy summer when he turned nine years old.

So no, he didn't have a woman, not at the moment, and he tried hard not to feel bad about that when his relatives teased him.

"You're thirty-six years old, ain't you sowed them oats yet?"

He had sowed his oats years ago, and at this stage in his life had no desire to share his bed or his body with just anyone. There were too many diseases out there, and the increase in AIDS had just about wiped out his libido altogether.

He hadn't been with a woman for over a year, and he was content for now with positioning the extra pillow just so against his back on nights when his king-size bed reminded him that he had no queen.

The trip would be a celebration of sorts, Campbell and her closest friends, Luscious, Macon, and her mother.

Everyone she cared about and loved.

But it hadn't come together quite the way she expected.

Laverna had plans to be in Aspen. Anita, with her mother in Tulsa. Porsche couldn't leave the kids, and she couldn't afford to take them, and no, she wouldn't allow Campbell to pay for them, absolutely not!

Luscious was afraid to fly, and Millie couldn't get the time off work, so that just left Macon.

She was overdue for a trip, a little rest and relaxation. She had done ten showings in seven different states in the past three months. Touring, keeping up with the increasing demand for special-order collages, and looking for a house had taken a toll on her both mentally and physically.

Campbell had been thrown into a whole new world, one that was different from what she expected. Yes, the grass always seemed greener on the other side until you actually got there and realized that it wouldn't be if it wasn't for the bullshit.

The life she was leading now had been a fantasy she'd allowed herself to lapse into in order to feel better about herself when she happened upon people she'd known as a child, some man or woman who had married into a well-to-do family or had acquired an Ivy league degree and was now making a six-figure salary. They all seemed to have Park Avenue smiles, high-powered jobs, and sixty-thousand-dollar vehicles that they parked in their Nassau County driveways.

She came across them quite often at the ticket counter. At least one a week, traveling on business, or worse yet pleasure, suntans still fresh on their skin from the last jaunt across the waters.

She tried not to hate them when they glanced and saw that her ring finger was empty but still asked, "Aren't you married yet?"

She wanted to tell them that she had had plenty of chances—well, at least two—but she wanted to get married for love and not convenience. She wanted to reel off the names of the men who had dropped to their knees and asked her for her hand forever, for always and for love; but she'd just smile and say, "No, not yet."

Because she'd been asked, but the love was one-sided, and she needed it to be all the way around.

And those old schoolmates, those people she tried so hard not to hate, they'd give her a pitiful smirk or that *Don't worry, it'll be all right smile*, that made Campbell feel two feet tall.

And now she was at the place, that golden peak that everyone strived to get to. And shouldn't she be happy? Yes, she should have been, but as the saying goes, Fame and money ain't nothing if you have no one to share them with.

Feeling bad, sad, and empty is what propelled her into the American Express travel agency. She had gone in with the full intention of just flipping through a brochure, but she walked out of there with two first-class tickets to Jamaica and two oceanfront suites at Beaches Negril.

It was a down payment on a house. That's how much she just charged on her credit card. Just looking at all those zeros made her want to puke.

But didn't her agent Dottie assure her that she deserved it, that the collages were selling like hotcakes and that two major publishing companies had inquired about using her artwork on book jackets?

Hadn't high-profile entertainers already commissioned her to do pieces for their summer and winter retreats?

What was ten thousand dollars when you had ten times that sitting in the bank and more constantly rolling in?

Millie had looked at her like she was crazy. "What the hell are you going to do in Jamaica during Christmas?"

"Lie on the beach and drink piña coladas."

"Macon, too?"

"Yes."

Millie was distraught. "We've never spent a Christmas apart," Millie had complained.

It was true—they hadn't spent a Christmas apart, not one—but Christmas had become a day filled with tension and too much wine.

Campbell wanted to start a different Christmas tradition, one that didn't end with Millie stumbling drunk to the front door, swinging it open, pointing to the spot where they stood, mother and daughter, adulteress and bastard child, and screaming about Fred destroying her life.

She couldn't have another Christmas like that. She wouldn't.

So she and Macon spent the holidays lying beneath the Caribbean sun and listening to the stories the palm tree leaves brushed against their trunks and the songs the wood doves cooed at dawn and dusk, and when the clock struck twelve announcing the arrival of the new year, Campbell hugged her daughter tight in her arms and reminded herself of everything she had in her life to be thankful for and tried not to think of that one thing she didn't.

"He called twice." Millie said as she examined the bottles of rum Campbell had brought back.

"Who did?" Luscious asked as she bit into a piece of the coconut candy Macon had given her.

"Donovan," Campbell said, and looked down at the piece of paper that Millie had written his name and number on.

"Well, do you know him?" Millie asked, and fingered the material of the T-shirt that had JAMAICA written across it in small aqua and pink letters. "You look like you trying to figure out who he is."

Campbell supposed she was a little mystified. It had been close to a month, and although she had tried to toss him out of her mind, he had haunted her since the first night they met.

"I know who he is. It's just that it's been a while since we've spoken."

"Well, I told him you were off in Jamaica."

"You always giving out too much information. Suppose Campbell didn't want anybody to know where she was?"

Millie made a face at Luscious and then looked back at Campbell. "Well, was it a secret?"

"No, Mom, it wasn't."

Millie stuck her tongue out at Luscious. She was in a playful mood. She was happy to have her daughter and granddaughter back home.

"See you later!" Macon yelled before rushing out of the front door.

"Can't that child stay put?" Millie complained. "She ain't been back in this country a good three hours, and already she's off running the streets. Did she even unpack?"

"Leave her alone. She's young; that's what young people do. She unpacked enough to give me these coconut candies." Luscious laughed.

"Which you don't need," Millie threw back at her.

"She misses her friends. She's back to school next week," Campbell interjected, but her eyes never left the paper, and her voice was barely a whisper.

Millie and Luscious exchanged looks.

"So, you going to call him or just stare at the message until he calls back?" Millie asked, and pulled a chair from the kitchen table.

"He'll call again if he's really interested," Luscious said, and popped another candy in her mouth.

Millie shot her a look. "The man has called twice. What more proof do you need to have to know that he's interested?"

Luscious just shrugged her shoulders.

Campbell stuffed the message into the back pocket of her jeans. "Anybody else call?" she asked, trying to pretend as if that small piece of paper meant nothing at all.

"Uhm, that real estate woman—Sierra, Sienna?" Millie fumbled with the name.

"You looking for a house, baby?" Luscious asked, her eyes flying open.

"Well, kind of."

Luscious narrowed her eyes and turned to Millie. "You ain't tell me nothing about that." And then back to Campbell. "You the one supposed to tell me to begin with."

Campbell had two too many mothers to answer to.

"I guess I just forgot," she said, and her thoughts drifted back to the message. *Twice, huh?* she thought to herself, and a small smile pressed against her lips.

Again, Millie and Luscious exchanged looks.

"Baby, I think you got a touch of sunstroke down there in Jamaica," Luscious said.

She waited three more days, waited until the sun-scorched skin on her nose and forehead had peeled away completely before she called him.

His hello was soft, and she'd thought that maybe she'd woken him from a nap; it was just past two on a Sunday afternoon.

"Hey, how you been?" he muttered, and then clearing his throat and speaking more clearly he asked, "How was Jamaica?"

There was never a lag, not one uncomfortable pause in that two-hour exchange. There had been laughter and questions, and by the time Campbell said good-bye, she was curled up and warm beneath her comforter, a big smile plastered across her face, and his "I'll come by tomorrow," still ringing in her ears.

He said he would be there by four, but by six he still hadn't shown up. Millie didn't say anything; she just watched her daughter move from the kitchen to the window, to the couch, and then back to the window.

The nervous energy that was spilling out of Campbell put Millie's nerves on end, and she got up and went to her room.

When the phone rang at seven, Campbell was in the bathroom wiping off her lipstick and thinking about tying up her hair for the night.

The anticipation and then the disappointment she'd experienced over the past few hours had drained her. And now she just felt tired.

She heard Millie tell the person on the end of the phone to hold on. "Campbell," she yelled from her bedroom. "Pick up the phone."

Campbell gave herself one last look in the mirror before clicking out the light and walking into her bedroom and picking up the phone. Millie didn't say it was Donovan, so Campbell thought it must be one of her friends.

"Hello," she said, her voice less than enthusiastic.

"Hey, what's up?" the voice asked.

Did her heart skip a beat? Was that a stupid grin spreading across her face?

"Hey you," she responded, and her voice climbed to a pleasant level.

"Sorry I didn't get there on time. I got caught up at work. Is it too late to come by now?"

"No, no." Campbell's response was quick, and she kicked her ankle for sounding too damn eager.

"Okay, I'm right outside."

"Okay," Campbell said, and moved to peek out the window. He *was* right outside, parked directly across the street from the house.

Campbell was down the stairs and at the door before he'd even taken the first step.

"Hi," she sang when she swung the door open.

He was filthy. Pants caked with oil, the Timberland boots he wore covered in grime.

Donovan saw the look on her face. "Work," he said. "Someone had thrown a television in the middle of the track. I had to stop the train, get out, and move it." He paused and looked down at his pants. "It's nasty down on those tracks," he added, and then laughed.

Campbell nodded.

"I won't come in. I can't even sit down, I'm so dirty. I just wanted to see you and say hello." And then that wide bright smile.

"You look good. I like your tan," he said, and Campbell couldn't help but blush.

"Oh, come on in. Don't worry about it." Campbell stepped aside to let him in while her mind worked on what she would have this man sit on.

Donovan stepped into the hallway and then followed Campbell into the living room, through the dining room, and into the kitchen.

"This is a great house. I love all of this old woodwork; they don't make houses like this anymore," he remarked as he stopped to run his finger across the intricate designs of the mantelpiece.

"Here," Campbell said as she pulled the wooden chair from the kitchen table. "I don't think your clothes will hurt this chair."

"Thanks," Donovan said, and sat down.

"Can I get you something to drink, eat, or both?" Campbell asked.

She was nervous again. Under the bright lights of the kitchen she felt like she was the sole performer on a large empty stage.

"No, thanks," Donovan said, and pushed the sleeves of his sweatshirt up to his elbows before resting his arms on the table.

Campbell remained standing, the small of her back pressed against the sink. The slight hum of the refrigerator was suddenly too loud. "Let me turn on the radio," she blurted and scurried from his view.

She felt like an idiot. Like a sixteen-year-old on her first date. He was just a man. *Just a man,* she told herself as she fumbled with the dials on the stereo system.

Donovan just shook his head.

Maxwell's "Fortunate" came blaring out of the speakers. Campbell turned the sound down two notches and came back to the kitchen.

"I love this song," Donovan said, and began to rock his head to the music.

"It is a great song." Campbell said, and reluctantly took the seat across from him. "Are you sure I can't get anything for you?"

Donovan didn't respond; he just waved his hand. "Love songs are my favorite. What about you?" He looked directly at her when he asked the question, and Campbell was caught like a deer in headlights when she looked into his eyes.

Is this how it started? She couldn't remember because she had not been attracted like this to someone in a long time. This must be how it started. The sudden loss of breath and the on and off again sound of your heart in your ears. Words caught in your throat and the sudden urge to lick your lips. Wanting to look away, but wanting more just to reach across the table and place your hand on some part of him.

Is this how it began?

"Yes," she finally said. "Love songs are my favorite, too."

He stayed little more than an hour. The house was warm, and he asked if Campbell would mind if he removed his sweatshirt. She didn't and tried not to watch as he pulled the material over his head. He had on two more T-shirts beneath that, but now his arms were bare, and Campbell could see the strength in them.

He thought maybe they could get together on Sunday.

"That would be great," Campbell said. She was going out of town tomorrow, but would be back on Friday.

It was just Monday, and as she walked him to the door she could already feel the anticipation building in her.

"You can call me, you know?" he teased her. "I just get so caught up with work," he started, and then tilted his head a bit and changed course. "I just think I'm the type of man who needs a little jump-start when it comes to this. I've been by myself for a while, you know. I've been out of the game for a while, you know?"

Campbell knew. She just nodded her head.

Donovan looked up at the sky and bristled as he stepped out into the cold night. He was on the third step before he turned and faced her again. He just looked at her. It wasn't a blank stare, but Campbell couldn't read his face.

He started back up the stairs, and Campbell almost took a step backwards when he was standing in front of her again. Standing this close she could smell the cologne he'd dabbed on his neck that morning.

He reached down and took her hand in his.

Campbell felt the corners of her mouth twitch as he slowly brought her hand up to his face and then bent his head and gently kissed the soft middle of her palm.

"Good night, Campbell," he said.

Campbell believed that she had offered him the same. She knew her lips were moving, but wasn't sure that anything had come out.

She remained in the doorway until his car turned the corner, and only then did she move her eyes to the place on her palm that was still warm from his lips.

She closed her hand into a tight fist and pressed it against her heart.

February

It'd been a little over a month, and Campbell was still touring and Donovan working long hours and most weekends, so they found little time to get together, but made up for it with telephone calls that went on for hours.

Sometimes when Campbell was on the computer, working, thoughts of Donovan would overwhelm her, and she would shoot off an e-mail to his cellular phone that said HI or HAVE A NICE DAY, some simplistic message that would let him know he was on her mind.

Their relationship was still in its infancy, and Campbell fought to keep it there as long as possible, even though what she was feeling already had her dressed in ivory and walking down the aisle.

She'd been burnt on more than one occasion.

But two days before Valentine's Day she found herself standing in front of the Hallmark store, staring in at the red-and-pink display of cardboard hearts, wrestling with the idea of whether she should buy a card for Donovan.

She walked out with a glossy four-by-six white card that held a small pink heart at its center. On the inside, in tiny black letters, it said simply, HAPPY VALENTINE'S DAY.

The winters were growing shorter.

Over the years Donovan had noticed that the heat of summer reigned well into October. The turning of the leaves reminded everyone that autumn had begun, but sweaters and lined jackets still lingered inside dark dresser drawers and hall closets.

Winter's chill took hold only in December, a week or so before the Christmas spruces and evergreens were chopped from their trunks and crammed into empty lots or lined at attention along sidewalks with large FOR SALE signs prominently displayed before them.

Before January reached its center, the days started to grow long again, and every now and then the warmth of a September day would find its way into that first month of the year.

Those days, those warm, out-of-place September days, made Donovan uncomfortable. He preferred the cold weather; the chill kept his mind clear, his thoughts clean.

On days when the temperature moved above sixty, he found himself thinking about Clyde, thinking about him so hard that Clyde became the voice of his thoughts.

Winter used to be his saving grace. The longest season of the year. The longest period of time when Donovan could forget about what was so unforgettable.

But now winter came in dribs and drabs and Clyde most all of the time.

But for now, February was going along just fine.

Blusterous mornings and deep-freeze evenings. Everyone dressing in layers, gloved and scarved. For now, things were going just the way they should.

Clyde was still a slow murmur at the back of his head, and thoughts of Campbell occupied the Clyde-free space at the forefront of his mind.

He took her for dinner at a small Italian place a friend of his had recommended.

The space was quaint, with ceramic-tiled floor, stucco walls with niches brimming with flowers, candles, or both. The small round tables were covered in red cloth, each adorned with a cluster of tiny flickering candles.

After dessert, just before Donovan called for the bill, Campbell had slid the Valentine's Day card across the table toward him. Donovan had blinked and then smiled before picking it up.

He tore the envelope open and read the contents of the card. Campbell warmed as she watched his smile broaden.

He looked up at her, and his eyes sparkled. "That was sweet," he said, and Campbell giggled at the sound of the word *sweet*.

"Well," she said, and dropped her eyes a bit, "you're a sweet guy." She laughed.

Donovan had looked at her for a while and then stood up, walked over to her, and kissed her lovingly on the cheek and then the curve of her neck. "Thank you," he whispered in her ear.

When they left, bellies full and Campbell's head swimming from the wine, she looped her arm through Donovan's to steady herself, but more to feel his closeness.

They made their way down the street, Campbell not quite staggering, but walking out of time and giggling when her full hips knocked into Donovan's narrow ones.

It was still early when they rolled over the Brooklyn Bridge.

Just after eight. Donovan looked over at Campbell as she gazed out the window, absentmindedly twisting one of her locks.

"Do you want to go home?" he asked.

"Huh?" Campbell uttered, dragging herself out of her musing.

"Are you ready to go home?" he repeated.

"No, not really," Campbell said, and tried to straighten her posture. She realized she was a little more than tipsy. "So where do you want to go?"

Donovan didn't say anything for a while. He checked the clock on the dashboard. Grammy would be out of the house by now, he thought, and on the bus to Atlantic City.

"Do you want to come by the house?"

"Okay, sure," Campbell said, not wanting to sound too excited. She'd never been inside his house.

The apartment was an L-shaped two bedroom with stark white walls that were bare except for the two framed Jacob Lawrence prints.

The plants stunned Campbell: large palms in each corner of the living room and colorful pots filled with cacti lined up along the base of the wall.

On the low glass table in front of the couch sat a clear bowl brimming with fragrant potpourri. Arranged around it were colorful scented candles that looked as if they'd had plenty of use.

A large-screen television took up the far right corner of the room, and in the far left, a stereo component set.

"Let me take your coat," Donovan said after Campbell had taken in everything.

She could tell he was nervous. Campbell just smiled.

"Would you like something to drink?" he asked as he pulled a wooden hanger from the hall closet. "Some wine?" he added before shutting the door. "Or have you had your fill of that?" he teased, and then let out a small laugh.

"I'll just have some water," Campbell said as she settled herself down on the couch.

"Don't you want to see the rest of the place?"

"Oh, of course," Campbell said, and pulled herself back to her feet.

She followed Donovan down a long narrow hall. "That's the bathroom," he said, and gave the door a little shove. It was small, but the skylight with the hanging plant beneath it and the green and white tiles on the wall gave it an airy feel.

"This is the extra room," Donovan said, pointing to the room directly across from the bathroom. Campbell peeked in and saw that he had the space set up with weights and a computer. The walls were covered with movie posters and shelves teeming with model cars.

"I collect that stuff," he said, a bit of bashfulness in his voice.

They moved four more steps down the hallway.

"This is my room," he said, and flicked the light switch on the wall.

It was a cozy room with a double-size bed, nightstand, and chest of drawers with multicolored bottles of cologne arranged neatly on its top. And a nineteen-inch television rested on a stand beside the dresser.

On the floor to the left of the bed, a dozen or so pairs of sneakers were neatly lined up. Behind that line were about six pairs of Timberland boots.

Campbell had been in quite a few bachelor pads, and most of the time they seemed to be unorganized or just plain junky. This house had an almost feminine order about it.

"Wow, you're neater than I am," Campbell said as she made her way back to the living room.

Donovan laughed. "No, not really. My grandmother comes

up here once a week and cleans up for me. Today was that day," Donovan yelled from the kitchen.

Campbell's eyebrows went up. "Oh," she murmured.

They started out sitting up on the couch, chatting about small things as Donavan roamed through the hundred-plus satellite stations he had.

Finally he settled on an old favorite of his, *The Color Purple*. He said as he slipped his shoes off and tossed them aside, "Do you like this one?"

"It's my all-time favorite." Campbell said, and stole a glance at her watch.

"Go on, make yourself comfortable," he said as he moved the crystal bowl and candles aside and propped his feet up on the table.

Campbell slipped off her boots and curled her legs beneath her on the couch.

They watched in silence until Campbell realized that Donovan was snoring softly. His head was resting on the back of the couch, and his lips were parted a bit. She thought he must be dreaming, because his eyeballs moved rapidly back and forth beneath his eyelids.

She just watched him for a while, struggling to keep the smile that tugged at her lips at bay. She wanted to touch him, stroke his cheek, and run her fingers down his neck and over his bulging Adam's apple.

His snoring became louder. He was out for the count. Campbell looked down at her watch. It was getting late.

Should she wake him? It was obvious he was dead tired. The thought of drawing him from his slumber and dragging him back out into the cold to take her home made her feel guilty.

Maybe she could take a cab home?

Maybe she should stay?

The last thought was more appealing to her.

"Hey, hey," she whispered softly as she gently shook Donovan's shoulder.

Donovan woke with a start. "Huh?" he said, and looked wildly around him before finally finding Campbell's smiling face. "Damn, I'm sorry. Did I fall asleep?" His voice was thick with slumber as he rubbed the sleep from his eyes.

"Yeah, you did," Campbell said, and reached for her boots.

Donovan looked at the television and then down at Campbell's feet. "Whatya doing? The movie is not over yet," he said before standing and giving his body a hearty stretch. "Are you in a hurry to leave me or something?"

Campbell was blushing. When he stretched, his sweater rose up a bit, and she'd been treated to his belly button, an innie.

"No, no," she said, averting her eyes.

"Relax. When the movie is over, I'll take you home. Okay?" he said, and slapped playfully at her thigh.

Seeing that part of him had ignited something inside her. The muscles in her thighs tensed, and her mouth went dry. *Jesus Christ*, she thought to herself, *has it been that long?*

She tried to gather herself and would have been successful in doing so if Donovan hadn't done what he did next. He walked off to his bedroom and changed into a loose net jersey and a pair of sweats. She could see his washboard stomach, broad chest, and powerful biceps through the cotton.

Campbell sighed.

"Do you mind?" he said as he picked up the pillow and dropped it on Campbell's lap.

"Uhm . . ." Campbell raised her arms in the air. She had no idea what it was he was about to do.

Donovan sat down on the couch and then slid sideways until

his head was resting on the pillow. He lifted his legs and swung them over the arm of the couch. "Thanks," he mumbled.

Campbell looked at her arms and hands, still suspended in midair. What was she supposed to do with them? If she lowered them, they would have to rest on some part of his body. Some part.

She felt like an idiot, sitting there, hands level with her face, fingers looking at her. She had no other choice. She would have to lower them, she would have to touch him. . . .

Slowly, she placed her left hand on his shoulder and the right on his head.

She waited, but there was no objection from him. She listened to his breathing. It remained the same. Felt for any rejection from his body. There was none.

It started slowly. Her index finger lightly gliding over his curls, the other fingers steadily joining in until her whole hand was stroking his head.

It felt good. The movement of her hand, the rhythm of his breathing.

She felt a murmur in her chest and cocked her head, trying to understand what it was that was building inside of her. She realized she was humming, not the "Over the Rainbow" song she normally turned to when she was sad, lonely, or afraid, but the nursery rhyme she would hush Macon with when she was small and wrapped up in the most loving place she could be, Campbell's arms.

"Hush little baby, don't you cry . . ."

The movie was over, but Campbell was too comfortable to move, and she didn't want anything to disrupt the warm feeling of contentment washing over her.

Yes, she thought to herself as she leaned her head back into the couch and closed her eyes. *Yes, this is how it begins.*

*　　*　　*

She woke with a start. She'd been dreaming about Pat.

They were sitting on a beach that was empty except for the two of them. No palm trees or salty mounds, just white sands that went on forever behind them, and in front of them a raging aqua sea.

Campbell was confused—there wasn't a cloud in the sky, yet the sea before them behaved as if it were caught in the winds of a violent storm.

She thought that Pat looked peaceful, unconcerned with the tide that was creeping closer and closer to them. Not disturbed by the waves that climbed higher and higher and then slammed down brutally against the shoreline.

"What is this place?" Campbell asked Pat.

Salt crystals sparkled like diamonds against her black skin, her lips cracking and drying beneath the sea spray that settled on them.

"Things aren't always as they appear," Pat whispers.

When Campbell's eyes fly open, it's her heart that's pounding in her ears and not waves, the sun in her dreams is the bright overhead light of the living room, and sitting beside her is Donovan.

"We fell asleep." He yawns. "What time is it?" he asks, and drags his hands across his face.

"Two," Campbell says, twisting her wristwatch into place and then bending over to reach for her shoes.

"Damn," Donovan utters. He watches her thoughtfully as Campbell grabs a boot, and then he touches her knee.

"Do you want to stay? I mean I have to get up in four hours, anyway. Work. I have to be up by six."

The words come in pieces that are mostly true, but what is definite is that he wants her to stay because he enjoys her closeness. It's been a long time for him; he wants to touch her without the bother of clothing.

Campbell isn't prepared for this. No sexy bra or lacy panties. She scours her memory—did she even lotion her legs or those areas on her sides that always seem to scale in the winter?

"If you don't want to, I'll take you home," he says when her answer takes too long to come.

Campbell finds the other boot. "No, no, just call me a cab. I'll be fine."

She wants to stay with him in the worst way. Wants to curl into him and run her hands across his stomach, kiss the back of his neck, and inhale the curls on his head.

But she imagines Millie's face, the long disapproving stare she would wash her with when Campbell walked through the door in the morning after spending a night with a man she'd known for only three months, a man Millie hadn't even met yet.

She'd call Campbell her father's child. "Well, you're certainly your father's daughter," she would spit.

Campbell knew it; she'd been in that situation before. She was a woman living in her mother's house, but she would forever be a child beneath Millie's roof.

"I can't put you in a cab at this hour."

What was he afraid of? She was a grown woman, for chrissakes!

"If I stay, how will you see me in the morning?" Campbell tosses the question at him out of nowhere.

Donovan was bent over his knees, lacing up his own boots. He turned his head slowly toward her. "The same way I see you now." His face was serious, his words sober and honest.

The moment was too grave; Campbell needed to take some of the weight off it. "You stay on your side of the bed." She laughed and kicked off one boot. "And I'll stay on mine."

He gave her a pair of basketball shorts and a T-shirt to sleep in. She cleaned her teeth as best she could with her finger and toothpaste before climbing into bed beside him.

Tucked beneath the heavy comforter, Campbell lay on her back, wide awake, staring at the shadows on the ceiling and listening to the hum of the electric clock on the nightstand by her head, waiting for him to touch her.

Donovan was on his stomach, his arms hidden beneath the pillow his head rested on, his breathing slow and even.

Is he asleep! Her mind screamed.

The comforter settled in the space between them, a space large enough to fit another human body. Was it possible to feel lonely in a bed with another person? She supposed it was.

Frustrated, she turned onto her side and stared into the darkness until she fell asleep.

Donovan got cold feet as soon as he suggested she stay.

It was a possibility—a small one, but a possibility just the same—that he wouldn't be able to perform. It had happened in the past. His body would be willing, but his mind wouldn't be there. His mind would retreat into the basement, and then soon after, his body would follow.

It was embarrassing, and he couldn't stand the look that would spread across a woman's face when it happened. The pity, most times anger.

He would have to be content with just having her there, he thought to himself before sleep took him over. Maybe next time.

By the time four o'clock rolled around, Campbell was in a deep sleep and Donovan was climbing out of one.

He shifted positions and his arm ended up on Campbell's waist.

It startled him, and he had to concentrate for a moment before the evening's events floated back to him.

He lay there that way, arm resting on her, his eyes gliding over her locks, which were spread out like a fan on the pillow. He listened to her breathing and felt the bed vibrate when she rubbed her feet together.

He moved his hand from her waist and reached out to her locks. They were soft, and he pulled them to his nose and inhaled the sweet oil she'd rubbed on them earlier that day.

He moved closer to her. His hand found her waist again, and he squeezed the soft flesh there. He was against her, one leg thrown over her thigh, penis pressing against her behind.

Campbell stirred and placed her hand on top of his. Their fingers entwined.

They stayed that way for a while, fingers entangled, his heart beating against her back, before she turned to face him and ran her fingers over his lips. Her eyes remained closed, but her lips found his eyelids, the bridge of his nose.

His hands fell on her breasts and began caressing them.

They moaned together.

His breath became labored as he pulled the shirt over her head and kissed her neck and the wide space between her breasts. He wanted to suckle her, but she would have to deal with the rhythmic rubbing of his rough palms for now. He was exploring the places behind her ears, the hairline of her forehead, her cheeks and chin.

Campbell pulled at his waist.

Finally, her nipples lay against his tongue and the roof of his mouth.

She was on fire.

"Donovan." She called his name when his hands slipped down between her legs.

The shorts were off and down around her ankles before she could utter another word. Donovan climbed on top of her and showered her face with kisses.

Campbell was drowning, drowning in the sea of Donovan and loving the sweetness of it.

It was her turn to undress him. She pulled his T-shirt over his head and kissed his baby-smooth chest. She gently pushed him off her and climbed on top, grabbing the waist of his sweatpants and easing it down off his lean hips.

She bent and kissed the space below his navel, and his body quivered and he whimpered. She could tell it had been a while for him, too, and she let experience and lust guide her over his body.

Donovan held on like a man dangling from a ledge. His fingers gripped Campbell's shoulders as her tongue touched every inch of him. When he finally eased inside her, he felt his eyes fill with water. Was it supposed to feel so right, so perfect?

Campbell pulled him deeper and deeper. She wanted him to touch that part of herself that hadn't been touched in years. She wanted to consume him and keep him with her forever.

He slid in and out of her like a slow bow over the tight strings of a cello, and they made music together when their bodies shuddered and exploded.

Lying there, breathless, warm, and full, both Campbell and Donovan were certain—completely confident, in fact—that this was indeed how it began.

Campbell jumped when the clock went off and was up and searching for her panties through the tangle of sheets and comforter by the time Donovan stirred.

"Hey?" a groggy Donovan whispered, his hands stretching out toward Campbell. "What are you doing?"

Campbell slipped on her panties. "Well, getting dressed. You have to get to work, right?"

Donovan sighed. "Well, damn, a brother would like to cuddle," he said, and pulled the covers around him.

Campbell stood watching him for a while. She was being adult about the whole thing. They'd both wanted something and had gotten it. It was just sex, right? Sometimes it was just sex.

She'd needed that, but what she wanted was something else. She couldn't be the only one wanting something—she'd been that woman in the past.

They were both adults, and as adults she should be able to be up front with him.

"Look, Donovan," she began.

"Hey, I know. You've been hurt, right? Well, so have I. Was this all about sex? No, no, it wasn't," he said, and pulled the comforter back and patted the sheet. "Come on. Just for a little bit."

Campbell sighed and climbed back in beside him.

"I'm not into casual sex, Campbell," he said as he pulled her to him. "I passed that stage a long time ago."

They lay there together for a long time, wrapped in each other's arms, lost in their separate thoughts.

"Donovan," she said, pulling away from him and sitting up. "You need to know something about me."

Donovan's heart skipped a beat. Her face was so serious, he felt his body tense.

Campbell took a deep breath. "You need to know that words mean everything to me."

Donovan raised himself up on one elbow; with his free hand he reached out and touched her forearm. "I mean what I say, Campbell. I'm not going to hurt you, ever."

Campbell believed him, believed him with everything she had in her, and she stepped off that cliff of safety she'd been balancing at the edge of for so many years and fell headfirst in love.

March

For Campbell, being in love was like being thrown into some type of sweet madness. Donovan on her mind at night before she fell asleep and there again when she opened her eyes.

Donovan slipping between her thoughts when she tried to work, read, or put on her clothes—she'd find herself standing before the mirror, pants, skirt, or shirt in hand, a whimsical grin across her face and no mind at all to guide her in dressing.

Campbell spending time replaying the words that passed between them, the easy silences when only his breath could be heard. Campbell thinking now that maybe she could write songs. Scribbling down words to the music that belonged to her and Donovan alone, music that her heart thumped out inside her whenever they were together.

She's started a collage for them, adding a picture at the end of each week. There are hearts and wineglasses. Snow and moonlight. Clefs and more hearts. Two aged smiling faces, foreheads pressed together. The center is stark white, the words that need to be there have not found her yet.

Maybe it will be, Will you marry me? She giggles at the thought and realizes quite suddenly that Donovan is religion to her. She folds her hands and bows her head.

She'd asked for him.

Had asked the Lord to send her someone she could love, someone who would love her back. But that prayer, that selfish request, had been at the bottom of her *God, please could you?* list.

Before Donovan, she'd convinced herself that she'd had her happiness. When she'd had it, she didn't know, but weren't we so often wrapped up in what was wrong in our lives that we were blind to all the good?

Shoot, she had her eyesight, both feet, and two hands.

Wasn't that enough?

She supposed it should have been, but wouldn't life be even more delicious if she could use her sight to gaze on one she loved, her feet to get to him, her hands to hold his?

Yes, it would have been nice. But she put that prayer behind health, food, and shelter, and when the loneliness became over-whelming and that biting desire bit down a little too hard for her to bear, she showered.

There, closed away behind the plastic curtain of daffodils and sunflowers, beneath the rush of water, no one could hear her weep, and so nobody could hear her pain.

She'd asked Donovan once, right out of the blue, why it was he decided to come with Elaine to meet her.

He'd looked off somewhere behind her before bending down and pressing his forehead against hers; their lips had brushed lightly, and then he said, "The angels heard your prayer for a soul mate."

His answer had pleased her.

Things were coming together quite nicely. She had an intelligent, healthy, and beautiful daughter, a successful career, a wonderful man, and two weeks ago when she stepped behind the double glass-and-mahogany doors of a three-story Victorian on Cranberry Street in Brooklyn Heights, she experienced the same feeling of contentment that came over her when she sat down to create, held Donovan's hand, or looked into her daughter's eyes.

This was the way things were supposed to be.

Donovan hadn't really gone searching for it. Campbell had given him the address. He hadn't even written it down, but for some reason his memory had held on to the name of the street.

Cranberry.

It was in Brooklyn Heights, a corner Victorian enclosed by a wrought-iron gate.

Just across the Hudson River was Manhattan; those homes, he knew for sure, those homes went for a million or more.

He hadn't realized that Campbell was making that type of money. I mean, it was easy to forget—she still lived at home with her mother, cut coupons, and did her own hair and nails, didn't even have her own telephone line or own a car.

She just didn't fit the profile, and so when she'd announced that she'd found a home and Donovan had asked where and she had told him, he laughed at her, saying that he thought she was mistaken. She had to have the wrong street name.

Campbell had twisted her lips up. Was it Cranberry Street?

She pulled the sheet of paper from her pocketbook. The name and telephone number of the realtor were written beneath the the address of the house.

"I'm right, it's Cranberry Street."

He'd come upon it quite by accident and had screeched to a

halt when he saw the gate and the green-and white door she said was the only part of the house she didn't like.

It was wide, with floor-to-ceiling windows. The stone steps leading up to the entranceway were grand, to say the least, broad and sweeping, and there were columns at the top of the staircase. Columns!

He parked his car and climbed out to get a better view. The house was just as long as it was wide, taking up more than a quarter acre and still leaving ample yard space.

Donovan grabbed hold of the gate and pressed his head against the cold metal. Were those fruit trees and a brick grill large enough to roast a whole pig?

He felt something in his stomach flip.

Jealous?

No, no, of course not, he told himself.

Aren't you happy for Campbell, her success, and what it is affording her?

Yes, yes, he cautioned himself as he climbed back into the car and shoved the key into the ignition.

Well, then, what's that feeling stirring in your gut, nudging at your ribs, tapping at your . . . manhood?

Nothing.

Inadequacy!

The word made him jump, and he pressed down too hard on the clutch, and the car stalled.

That's just stupid.

Is it? What the hell could you possibly give a woman who makes six times more than you do? You've just seen the outside of that house. Do you know what it looks like on the inside?

She told you, didn't she?

Hardwood floors, fifteen-foot ceilings, fireplaces—all working. Three—count them—three bathrooms.

Shut up.

What could you contribute if you moved in with her? If you married her?

Donovan looked back at the house and then drove home and climbed into bed. When Campbell called that night, he let the phone ring until the answering machine clicked on.

"Hey, babe. Where are you? Well, I'll try your cell phone. I miss you."

He pulled the blanket over his head and closed his eyes against the chiming sound of his cell phone. He needed some time, he thought to himself. He needed to think.

April

Earlier weeks had been damp and fraught with the stench of standing garbage. Sanitation went on strike on April Fools' Day. But now two weeks in, the dispute had been settled and the skies were clear and the harsh March winds that had found their way into April had dissolved into gentle breezes that carried the scent of blossomed things through open windows.

She'd started packing.

Winter clothing, the china set that had been given to her as a gift when she returned a forgotten wallet to a passenger. Sheets and towels that she'd purchased over the years at department store white sales.

There were boxes everywhere—underneath her bed, lined up along the walls of her bedroom, and stacked hill high in Macon's room.

Campbell had been so wrapped up in everything else and

Donovan that she hadn't had time for her friends, so when Anita called and requested her presence, she'd agreed.

"Do you think you could give a sister a little attention?" Anita's voice came crystal clear through the receiver.

Campbell let out a small guilty laugh.

"You're a big-time artist now and can't seem to find any damn time for your friends, huh?"

That stung a bit, even though Campbell knew that Anita was being sarcastic.

"Danube, brunch tomorrow at three, okay?"

Campbell agreed and hung up.

It's too cool to sit outside. The warmest part of the day is between eleven and two; after that a chill starts to creep in, so they take a table near the large pane window.

They sit there, three smiling faces with painted lips and shadowed eyelids, watching Campbell as she walks toward them, smiling, floating. They greet her with kisses that leave streaks of lipstick on her cheeks, and they sip on their water until she's settled herself and reaches for the cloth napkin.

They're patient for those short moments it takes for her to decide on a drink and appetizer. They're patient because they have her for an entire meal and possibly dessert. They won't mention the spread in her hips or the way her skirt hugs her backside, the fullness of her bosom or the plumpness of her face.

They know the weight gain is due to the tranquillity that comes along with fresh love, those languid hours a new couple shares when they're getting to know each other. Evenings spent consuming rich meals, nights on bar stools laughing and touching each other in between sips of their drinks and comments to the bartender. And then the nights, long nights of pleasing one another, discovering what makes the other quiver and cry out.

When Campbell finally rests her elbows on the table and folds her hands beneath her chin, they know without even asking that she is in that warm pink place they equate with love and happiness.

Her skin is glowing and her eyes sparkle, and have they ever seen her makeup applied so perfectly, her hair just right?? Is that a French manicure, and was she tweezing her eyebrows now?

Anita is the first to speak. And it is expected of her. "I bet you're even shaving your legs." She is the most outspoken of the group. Tall and stocky with dark skin, wide eyes, and a quick tongue.

"And probably someplace else," Laverna interjects slyly with her Mickey Mouse voice.

Porsche laughs. "Girl, I don't think we've ever seen you like this."

"Oh, please." Campbell says, and blushes a bit.

"Oh, please, *my foot*," Anita shrieks. "Now it's one thing not seeing you. That's fine—shit, we're all busy. But damn it, girl, we can't even get you on the phone—"

"Yeah, I called the other night and she was on the phone with *him*." Porsche cuts Anita off.

"I—," Campbell starts, but they're not done with her yet.

"Ain't you 'bout ready to close on the house?" Porsche asks.

"Yes," Campbell says.

"Well, that's going to be a waste of money and space because you ain't never going to be there. As it stands now, you're always over at that man's house."

"I am not always—"

"Well, maybe he's going to move in with her," Laverna says, and they all look at each other and then at Campbell and wait.

Campbell nibbles on her bottom lip. She *had* thought about them being together in that house. Tearing away the awful wallpaper, picking out new tiles for the bathroom, new light fixtures for the hallways, a throw rug for the parlor.

Hadn't she imagined them curled up in front of the fireplace, her cooking breakfast for him, sending him off to work in the morning and welcoming him home again at night?

She'd imagined all of it.

"No, we're not going to live together," Campbell finally says, and just the words, hearing them out loud, make her heart sink a bit.

The women sigh.

"Well," Anita says as she messes with the napkin in her lap. "I think it would be too soon, anyway."

She was the oldest of the four. Danube was her restaurant. She'd had it for eight years. She was married to her business. It's the only thing in her life that she could depend on, she said. All the women knew that it was the only thing in her life that she could control completely.

Men, well, that was another story.

She blamed them. Blamed them for not having the balls to deal with a strong, independent woman.

"Black men," she would say, "black men have a severe problem. They're easily intimidated by a strong black woman. I think it's in their biological makeup. I believe, ladies, that I am going to have to cross the color line if I'm ever to find true love."

But she never had and now at 38, she was successful and alone.

Porsche rolls her eyes at her and then places her hand on Campbell's arm. "There ain't no schedule where love is concerned," she says, and shoots Anita a sharp look. "It happens when it happens. If it feels right, go with it."

Anita grumbles.

Porsche was the middle woman of the group. Petite, pecan-colored, and glamorous, and at the age of thirty-six, she'd been married for eighteen years and had given birth to four children.

Porsche believed in love, marriage, and family.

Laverna, the baby. Medium sized and fair skinned with close-cut hair and a jutting nose. She was attractive in the right light. Flat chested and all behind, men salivated when she walked past them.

Just thirty-four. She'd been in a relationship with a woman for more than six years now. Prior to that, she'd been heterosexual. "And apparently stapled to my forehead was a sign that read WANTED: ABUSERS, ASSHOLES, AND ADDICTS," she'd said on more than one occasion.

It was always the wrong man, but now, Porsche said, she had found the right woman.

"I knew I was in love with Debra the third time we slept together. We moved in with each other a week later. It's been six years," Laverna says as she polishes the teeth of her fork with her napkin.

Anita bristles and beckons the waiter over. "Evidently this fork is not clean enough for Ms. Thompson. Would you please get her another?" she says, her voice dripping with sarcasm.

Laverna just shakes her head. "I hate eating here," she jokes, and folds her arms across her chest.

"Look, Campbell, I love you and just don't want to see you get hurt. You're in a whole different position now. People are going to want to be with you for all the wrong reasons; it's going to be hard to figure out who wants to be with you for the right ones." Anita looks down at her hands and adjusts her thumb ring before adding, "Believe me, I know."

The women agree with that last statement.

"Be happy, but just be careful," Anita whispers in her ear when she hugs and kisses her good-bye.

May

They had discussed it on and off for a few weeks, and now Campbell was sitting across from him, beaming with excitement as she flipped through the dozen or so glossy colored brochures she'd spread across his kitchen table.

They all looked the same to him. White sand beaches, thatched-roof villas with four-poster beds draped in mosquito netting. Smiling black-faced chefs holding trays heavy with lobsters. A sunset, a low moon. All the same.

She'd been everywhere. He'd heard all the stories, and now she wanted to take him to those places so they could have stories that belonged to both of them.

He'd never been on a plane. Every vacation he'd ever taken, he'd gotten there by car. Except that one time when he accompanied Grammy on a train to Montreal.

He tried to seem enthusiastic, but his mind was on the toothbrush that had been sitting in the holder next to his for the past week. The nightgown hanging behind the bathroom door and the T-shirt, the one that belonged to him, the one that Campbell had dubbed her favorite and always slipped on when she knew she would be there for more than a few hours.

She was becoming a part of his space. Like the potted cacti and the prints on the wall.

It hadn't really bothered him too much in the beginning—he'd actually become quite used to her being there, missing her when she wasn't—but then he saw the house, and the toothbrush came a few days after that, and Grammy had made some comments, and all of a sudden he'd started feeling differently, started to feel trapped.

"Well, why haven't I met her yet?" Grammy's tone was filled with anger.

Donovan shifted. Daisy had asked him that very same question, but her voice had been soft, curious. Donovan has assured her that he would bring Campbell around soon enough. Daisy had just laughed. "Do you like her?" she'd asked.

"She's all right, I guess," Donovan had responded.

Daisy had laughed again. "You're blushing," she'd said before cupping his cheek. "She must be more than all right."

"Has your father met her?"

Donovan shook his head.

"Grammy?" Just saying her ex-mother-in-law's name made her wince.

Again Donovan shook his head.

Now Grammy was reading him the riot act.

"I mean, you sneak her in late at night; I hear her leaving early in the morning. *Decent* women visit men at *decent* hours of the day."

Donovan scratched at his chin and then looked thoughtfully at his fingernails. "I don't sneak her in, Grammy. It's just that she's busy, I work late, and its just seems to work out that way."

"Well, am I ever going to meet this, this"—Grammy was searching for the right word—"mystery woman?"

"Yeah, sure. Soon."

Grammy looked at him for a while. She was getting old, her knees were bad, she slept more hours in the day than a cat did. She was sure her days were numbered, reminded Donovan and Solomon of that fact every chance she got.

Sometimes, if she was feeling especially dramatic, she would even manage to squeeze out a tear or two while she pitied herself. "You don't love me anymore. You want me to go to one of those retirement homes, those jails for old people, that's what you want!"

Donovan would hush her, tell her that it wasn't true, hug her, and say that he was her good boy, her Donovan.

That's the way she wanted it to remain, but now this woman she'd never met was threatening the balance of what she'd worked hard at establishing. She'd seen the toothbrush, the nightgown on the back of the door, the empty pack of condoms in the bathroom trash bin. She'd seen it all.

"Well, what is it she does that keeps her so busy?"

"What?"

"Work. What type of work does she do?"

"Oh. She's an artist," Donovan said, and opened the refrigerator.

Grammy's eyesbrows went up. "Really?"

"Yeah," Donovan said, and reached for a can of soda.

"What does she paint?"

"She doesn't paint. She pieces bits and pieces of magazine and newspaper clippings together on a board," he said, and popped the tab.

Grammy was washing dishes. She turned the water off and shook her hands dry over the remaining dishes before placing them on her hips.

"What?" Grammy screwed her face up. "That's art?"

"Yeah."

"Well, what kinda art is that?"

"It's called collages." Donovan took a sip of soda and then peered down into the can.

"And she gets paid for these, uhm, collages?"

"Yep."

"Humph. Well, shoot, I could do that."

Donovan just shrugged his shoulders.

"Well," Grammy sounded, and moved over to the table and sat down.

She was quiet while she digested the information, swirled it around in her mind, and decided how she could use it to her advantage.

"You know," she began. Her voice low, her words even. "Those artsy types can be a bit strange. I think it's the drugs."

Donovan looked at her.

"Oh, yeah, the drugs is what helps them come up with all that crazy stuff that makes it art."

Donovan let go a little laugh and shook his head.

"I'm not saying that your friend . . . What's her name again?"

"Campbell."

"Oh, yeah. I'm not saying Campbell is one of them—a drug user—I'm just saying that's what some of them do."

Donovan just sighed.

Grammy shot him a sly look. "She, uhm, have children?"

"One. A girl."

"Oh, that's nice. Well, she'll probably not want any more—you know those career women don't have time for babies and bottles and such. There's always meetings and parties and stuff."

Donovan set the can of soda down on the table. He wanted children, and Campbell did seem to go out a lot.

"Yeah, those hoity-toity artsy-fartsy types drinking champagne and going to the country club." Grammy altered her voice to sound like a bad Robin Leach. "Caviar in the fridge. They've got sofas instead of couches, carports instead of garages." Grammy broke up with laughter at her wit. "The women are the worst. I think their husbands have to take their wives' last name!"

Another roar of laughter ripped through Grammy and bellowed in Donovan's ears.

"Well, hey, Donovan. I'm not saying that would be the case with you and, uhm, Campbell. I'm just saying," Grammy said as she wiped the tears from the corners of her eyes.

Grammy had gone on and on, and that combined with Clyde's voice always taunting him wasn't helping, not one bit.

Clyde seemed to come like the green things that budded on tree limbs and poked out from the earth. He came when the days began to yawn and stretch and the weather lost its chill and windbreakers and baseball caps replaced heavy coats and woolen hats.

He was the one who'd pointed out the toothbrush and the nightgown.

Look at that, Cappy! Looks to me like she's moving in. Marking her territory, boy. Just like a cat.

Shut up.

Just like a cat!

* * *

"So I was thinking that maybe we could do something for your birthday, take a trip to the islands. Barbados maybe or Saint Kitts?" Campbell said.

"I've got to see if I could get some time off," Donovan mumbled, and scratched at his neck.

Campbell looked up at him. Hadn't they had this conversation about his obsession with work? He'd agreed that he would cut back when the weather started to get warmer, had promised her the summer.

"When June and July hit, you're going to be sick of me, because all you're going to see is me," he'd said way back in March when twelve whole days had slipped by and they hadn't seen each other.

"It won't always be this way." Those were his words, and she believed them to be true. But they were well into May, and Donovan had worked every single weekend, Saturday and Sunday, for four weeks.

She had tried not to complain, not to whine, and not to remind him of his promises. "Well, do you think you could ask your boss on Monday, when you go into work?" she said.

Donovan pushed himself up from the table. "Yeah, sure."

She had to remind him three times, and with each reminder she could feel frustration climbing into her voice. Annoyance seeping into her words.

"I'll ask him today." "I forgot." "He's been out sick."

Excuses, that's all they were. He was unsure now. The weather was warm, and his thoughts were muddled. Clyde was talking to him all the time now.

"Well, did you ask?"

Donovan had gone right to bed when he came in from work. He was groggy when he answered the phone, and Campbell jumped all over him.

"Did you ask? I mean I want to book the flight and hotel before we lose the dates."

She hadn't even said hello. Donovan closed his eyes.

"How much is it?" That was the other thing. He kept thinking about the house. The furniture she said she'd ordered. Large expensive pieces for the bedroom and living room. This trip was probably going to cost a fortune.

Campbell was silent for a moment. "Baby, this is my birthday gift to you," she said, and her voice softened. "All you need to do is show up."

Is that what type of man you are Donovan? Kept? Grammy's voice echoed in his mind.

"I was asleep, Campbell. Let me call you back," Donovan said before hanging up the phone and pulling the covers over his head.

June

She can't quite remember when the disagreements began, the bickering over foolish things. The days on end when all Campbell felt was anger—and Donovan, relief that she wasn't speaking to him and he didn't have to hear that tone in her voice.

That time in the Tattoo Gallery was as close as she could gauge it. They'd had lunch in the Village and afterwards had decided to roam the streets, popping into and out of stores, just enjoying themselves and each other.

He'd been talking about getting a tattoo on his chest or maybe his forearm. They'd walked through shops that offered piercing and tattoos.

Campbell was teasing him, whispering in his ear that she'd get her nipples pierced if he'd do the same. He'd looked at her like she was crazy and then laughed until his sides ached.

At the last shop, the Tattoo Gallery, they'd stood side by side, flipping through the volumes of skin art resting on the counter, pointing out to each other pictures that appealed to them.

"Hey, how about this one?" Donovan nudged Campbell's arm.

Campbell leaned over and her eyes fell on a panther hiding in cover. "Umph, you don't want that. Panthers are incestuous animals," she'd quipped, and then pushed her book over to him and pointed to a picture of a penguin. "Penguins," she said in her softest baby voice, "Penguins mate for life."

Donovan hadn't appreciated that bit of information about panthers. He'd taken offense at it. Thought that she was ridiculing him, as if she knew what had happened to him as a boy.

After that, he'd become quiet. They'd left the city soon after that, and the drive home was tense. Campbell had opened her mouth numerous times to speak, but each time had decided against it.

Donovan's jaw was set and his eyes narrow as he cut recklessly in and out of traffic. Campbell was nervous, scared, and confused. She didn't know what she did to put Donovan in such a foul mood. She gripped the leather seat, and for the first time since Pat stepped off the platform, she began to hum.

Donovan had thought he'd heard right. A soft humming, a quiet drone that made him perspire and caused the hairs on the back of his neck to stand on end.

He glanced at her sideways and cocked his head a bit in her direction. He listened, and when he was sure about the tune, he jerked his head back and shifted into fifth gear.

He hated that damn song!

Even the happiest of couples fought, she told herself. They were just going through a rough patch. They had reached the six-month mark, the place where the road they'd been traveling mounted, and they had to adjust themselves, move into four-wheel drive, and work together to conquer the proverbial bump in the road.

He hadn't touched her in weeks, and one night when she came to him after having dinner with her agent, her head swimming from the champagne, her thighs yearning and aching to be wrapped around him, she'd invited him to shower with her and he'd declined. That was fine, she was still buzzing when she climbed into bed butt naked beside him.

He'd just lain there, clutching his pillow and staring at the television.

The champagne coursing through her veins would not allow her to be perturbed, and she pulled him onto his back and mounted him.

A log had more feeling than Donovan. He just folded his hands behind his head and turned his face back toward the television.

Campbell just sat there, staring at him until he finally acknowledged her. "I'm tired," was all he said, and gently pushed her off him.

She was too drunk to be hurt, but she was angry and finally fell off to sleep.

Hurt came in the morning when she woke shivering, her body curled into a ball, a thin sheet wrapped at her waist, and no Donovan. He had taken the comforter and pillow and spent the night on the couch.

That was in early May, and now it was the middle of June, and Donovan still hadn't touched her. The phone calls waned, and suddenly there was no time for dinner, movies, or even lazy hours spent in his apartment.

Just a rough patch.

But one day while she was sweeping the floor, a thought gripped her. *Could it be another woman?*

Campbell's stomach cramped.

She'd been through that before with Andre. She'd been in love with him, too, head over heels. He'd left her at his apartment and had gone to help a friend who was stuck out on the highway. "I'll be back in two hours, tops," he'd promised.

They'd been watching television in bed when the phone call came. "Okay," she'd said, thinking nothing of it. Andre was a good guy; he helped everyone.

She was fast asleep when he'd finally tipped through the door four hours later. He peeked into the bedroom before pulling the door in, not closed, just in a bit, and then he went into the bathroom.

The creaking bedroom door and the sound of the light switch being flicked on had roused her, and she'd climbed out of bed and made her way to the bathroom, just to speak to him, just to hear how everything had turned out.

There wasn't a fleck of grease on him. That was the first thing that struck her. He was as clean as he was when he'd left. The second was the trickle of water that was coming from the sink faucet, not enough to make a sound against the porcelain of the sink.

The third and final thing, which she always told herself should have been the first, was the dark portion of flesh that rested on the inside curve of the sink. It confused her at first and she had to rub at her eyes and blink before it finally all made sense.

Andre was washing his penis.

"What are you—?" she started to say, and then stopped. "Oh, my God," she uttered, and backed away from the bathroom.

The laugh followed. That inappropriate giggle that always seemed to blossom out of her when she was taken off guard.

She and Andre had been happy. Hadn't they?

Campbell shook her head against the implication of the memory.

No, what she and Donovan had was different. They belonged together. She believed it heart, mind, and soul.

But the thought still tugged at her mind.

She would never have believed that the problem wasn't another woman, just one dead man.

She called him twice. He wasn't home or was pretending not to be, and then she called his cell phone and still she did not get an answer.

She paced the floor.

Her head was beginning to hurt. Visions floating through her mind: Donovan lying next to another woman. Donovan kissing another woman. Donovan touching another woman.

She grabbed hold of her locks and tugged hard, as if pulling them out at the roots could pull the images from her head.

The phone rang, and she snatched it up. "Hello," she barked into the receiver.

"You called me?"

No hello or how you doing. Campbell was incensed. "Yes, I did. We need to talk, Donovan. I'm feeling a little confused right now, and I'm very angry—"

"You always angry." Donovan's voice was bored.

Campbell sucked in as much air as her lungs could hold. She didn't want to curse—she wasn't one to really use words like that—but he was taking her there.

She exhaled.

"Donovan," she started, a bit calmer now, "look, I just think we need to get some things out in the open—"

"Well, I'm listening." His voice was like ice.

That was it for Campbell. A rush of words, some she had rehearsed and others that had somehow found their way into her mouth, came rushing out, and when she was done, her hands were shaking and her eyes were wet and Millie was standing at her bedroom door with a concerned look on her face.

Campbell put her hand up. Millie backed away and with one last look pulled the door shut.

Donovan was laughing, he was actually laughing, and in between the laughter Campbell heard things like, "I do know other people." And, "I can't be under you twenty-four seven." And, "What the hell do you want from me?"

She had responses for everything he flung at her.

But the last statement, the one she took like a blow to her gut was, "The last time I checked, Campbell, we weren't married."

It was a silent undoing. No tears, just a total breakdown of her spirit.

She hung up the phone.

Seven days come and go, and Campbell tries to keep her mind occupied with the collage she's working on, the packing, and the swatches of paint she's considering for her bedroom and the kitchen.

She wants to call Donovan, needs to call him, but she doesn't. She knows what a junkie feels like now, because she's addicted to Donovan and she's trying to kick him, but it hurts everywhere.

Was this how it was with Andre?

No, she didn't go through anything like this. She had been more angry than hurt. She had left him and for good reason. She had had a reason. What was happening here, what was going down between her and Donovan, made no sense at all.

On the eighth day he called. His voice was low and apologetic. Campbell had the phone gripped so tightly in her hands, her knuckles were white.

"I'm sorry, Campbell. I've just been going through something. I didn't mean to take it out on you."

Campbell felt relief wash over her. It had been the hardest week of her life. She never wanted to go through it again.

"I'm sorry, too," she breathed, and then before he could respond. "Can we get together?"

He was silent, and for one desperate moment Campbell thought he was going to deny her again.

"Sure. I'll come by later."

Later never came. Instead, she got a phone call two hours after his promised arrival time.

"Listen, I got caught up. Can I come tomorrow?"

Campbell bit her lip. "Sure. Tomorrow, then."

It took three days for tomorrow to get there, and when he finally did come, Campbell was right back in the state of anguish he had dumped her into two weeks earlier.

"Donovan, I just need to know, is there someone else?" She blurted it out as soon as she swung the door open.

Donovan just blinked. "Can I come in first?"

Campbell stood aside.

They moved to the couch, Donovan wedging himself into the corner and as far away from Campbell as possible. But he couldn't escape those eyes, those eyes of hers weighed down with hurt.

He laughed because he was nervous, not because there was anything humorous about the situation.

Campbell's eyebrows flew up, and Donovan raised his hand to halt the fury he suspected she was about to fly into.

"There's no one else, Campbell. I'm just going through something is all," he said, and shifted uncomfortably. "I know I've been a little distant, but it's not you. It's me."

Campbell relaxed a bit. That was good. It wasn't her; it was him. That was good.

"I'm sorry that I've gotten you all upset."

Campbell ran her hands through her hair. She was relieved that they were finally communicating again.

"Well, I'm sorry I overreacted," she sighed.

She wanted to reach out to him, but something in his manner, in the way he remained in that tight corner of the couch, told her that he wasn't ready for her to touch him. That was fine—she would settle for his presence for now. For the moment, that would have to be enough.

"So are we still on for Saint Martin?"

They had settled on that island.

Donovan hesitated before answering. "Y-Yes." His response was barely audible.

Campbell cocked her head. "Are you sure?" If he said no he wasn't, she would die.

"Uh-huh," he said, and stood up. "I've got to get up early," he said, and brushed at his pants.

Campbell eyed him.

"Earlier than usual," he added, and shoved his hands inside his pockets.

Campbell accepted his reason, even though she felt he wasn't being completely honest with her.

When they got to the front door Donovan just said good-bye and started down the steps.

This was how the *other* thing began, she thought to herself.

July

The Federal Express package came on the third, and the flowers, large purple blossoms in a mauve vase, on the fifth, his birthday.

Both deliveries were from Campbell. The FedEx package contained his airline ticket. First class.

The flowers were embarrassing. Grammy had just made a face at him and shook her head and mumbled something he knew he didn't want to hear.

"I wish I could be there with you, Donovan." Campbell's voice came across in distressing threads that pulled at Donovan's scalp.

"I know."

There had been a last-minute inclusion in an art festival being held in Charleston. She had flown out that morning and would be there until the eighth. They were due to leave for Saint Martin on the ninth. "I'll just meet you in Miami for the connecting flight," she said.

"Uh-huh."

There was silence, and then they both started to speak at the same time.

"No, you go ahead," Campbell said, and pressed her cell phone against her ear.

"I was just going to ask you how the flight was and if you were having good weather."

Campbell smiled. "The flight was fine, just fine."

He was sounding a little bit more like himself. This trip will be good for him, for both of them. "It's so hot down here. But it's beautiful. Big old houses. We should come back together one day."

There was silence, and then Donovan cleared his throat before saying, "Yeah, we'll have to do that."

"Well, I have a two o'clock presentation, so I'm going to go. We'll talk later, then?"

"Sure."

"Okay, well, happy birthday again. I love you," Campbell said.

The "I love you" had come out as easily and as naturally as good-bye and it had felt good to say, Campbell thought to herself as she stuffed her cell phone back into her purse.

It felt right to say it.

Donovan moved the phone away from his ear and stared at the receiver.

His mouth had moved to respond, "I love you, too," but the words had clumped up at the back of his throat and he'd nodded instead.

He'd remained that way for a while, standing there, staring at the phone, trying to clear his throat of the words he'd never be able to speak to Campbell, and after more than twenty minutes and two glasses of water, he placed the phone back into its cradle and slid the plane ticket across the smooth wood of the kitchen counter and into the garbage.

She stood there long past the time American Airlines flight 44 departed. The agent at the desk announced the final boarding and then called her name.

She watched from the large glass windows as her bags were removed from the flight, and even when they changed the black-and-white signs on the board that informed the passengers that flight 65 to Chicago would be leaving from that gate, she still remained.

If she could have walked, she probably would have. But her legs were weak, and she knew that if she took one step away from that window, she would come apart at the seams and crumble right there on that standard gray airport carpet.

She'd called his house, and the computer voice on the other end advised her that the number had been changed. No further information was available.

She'd tried his cell phone, and all she got was a constant busy signal. She'd called AT&T cellular service and asked if they could check the number for her, and they did. It had been disconnected.

So she stood there, and the movie that was her short time with Donovan played over and over in her head, and with each scene, she pressed PAUSE and concentrated hard on his words, his touch, and his eyes, trying hard to understand what had happened between them.

There was nothing, nothing she could see that told her that things would end up like this. Not like this.

She probably would have remained there forever, hands pressed against the glass, staring at herself, but someone had picked up the phone and called security. "She's been here for like nine hours. I think there's something wrong with her."

There was something wrong indeed. She had had the rug pulled out from beneath her, the door suddenly slammed in her face—she had spread her arms out at her sides, closed her eyes, and fell backwards, more than sure that she could trust Donovan to catch her, and had hit the floor. *Blam!*

To the two burly-looking white men in blue uniforms and guns dangling from their waists, Campbell must have looked like a vagrant.

The crisp green linen suit she'd donned that morning was creased and so badly wrinkled it looked as if she'd slept in it.

The oil from her skin had sucked up all the makeup she'd applied that morning. There were remains of the copper-colored lipstick she favored trapped inside the creases in her lips, and dark circles beneath her eyes from that mascara that had been caught in the on-again, off-again tears she'd cried.

One man asked if she was ill while the other guard smiled smugly and tilted his hand to his mouth in a drinking motion. "Spent a little too much time at the bar, did we?"

No, she wasn't ill or drunk; she was just confused and hurt.

"Sorry," she'd mumbled at them, and shuffled around them and toward the sign that said EXIT—GROUND TRANSPORTATION AND BAGGAGE CLAIM.

December

Campbell stood in the window of her new home. The logs in the fireplace crackled behind her as she sipped her tea and watched her neighbors stroll up and down the streets.

Five months later, she was just starting to gain the weight back, answering the phone instead of allowing the machine to get it. Smiling sometimes and crying a little less often.

She supposed the therapist had had a lot to do with it.

Campbell had been ashamed to go, but she started thinking about Pat, understanding now what that pain must have been like for her and how much she needed to escape it, because Campbell felt the same way, and it scared her to know that there was more of her that wanted to die than to continue living each blessed day in sorrow.

For a long time it seemed as though there were nothing anyone could do. Not Millie, Macon, or Luscious, but they all kept watch over her those weeks she lay in bed, not wanting to bathe or eat, just sleeping, and in between the sleeping, the tears, so many tears.

"What happened? What can we do?" they asked, faces heavy with worry, hands busy rubbing her shoulder, tucking the comforter around her, rubbing her shoulder, touching her head for fever, and wiping her tears away.

Campbell had no answers for them. Could she say that this was all because of a man, because of love? That was too trifling a problem to have a total breakdown over.

But she had.

When her best friends came to see her, they had solemnly ascended the stairs but hurried to fix their faces with bright smiles outside Campbell's bedroom door. They rushed in, the flowers and balloons they carried with them making a racket.

Millie had tried to prepare them. First on the phone and then again when they stepped through the front door.

Smiles fell away, and their faces were suddenly long and eyes going wet just to look at her. Laverna had to grab hold of the bookshelf to steady herself, toppling the miniature ceramic penguins perched on its top.

Anita had been the first one to ease herself down onto the edge of the bed and pat Campbell's thigh. She looked at Campbell and shook her head as she ran her hand over the new blades of hair that were pushing up from Campbell's scalp.

Campbell had cut off her locks while she was still in Florida. Had stood in front of the mirror weighed down with grief and hollow, her mind wandering on Pat and understanding full well how her friend had felt on that day she stepped off the platform.

Campbell lightly ran the blade over her wrist.

Macon came to mind, and so did Millie and Luscious and her friends, and Macon again and Macon, Macon . . . only Macon.

In the end, she used the blade to cut away her hair, hacking it down to the scalp.

Anita stroked Campbell's head and then her cheek, running her finger along the dark half moons beneath her eyes. Those half moons made her look like a cancer patient, and in some strange way, Anita supposed she was.

Campbell wouldn't look at Anita or any of the women; she just lay there, motionless, staring at the wall.

Anita slipped off her expensive silk jacket, kicked off her shoes, and climbed into bed beside Campbell, wrapping her arms tight around her.

The others followed suit, each finding a small space to rest in and some part of Campbell to hold.

They prayed.

They'd all been there in some part of that shadowed place Campbell had climbed into. They knew and understood that a man *could* do this to a woman, and there was nothing trifling or shameful about it.

Epilogue

Eventually the pain ebbed away, and the grief faded. The anger that followed was cutting but brief, and for that Campbell was thankful.

The love she had for him never changed, never shifted or waned, just remained lodged inside her, wrapped around her heart.

She still looks for him behind the smoked glass windows of Benzes and in the framed rectangular glass of the motorman's chamber.

Her heart still hopes when the phone rings and her eyes search for his smile in crowds.

She has a better understanding about love and the paths God and the universe have laid out for her, and it allows Campbell to muse that perhaps she and Donovan will meet again in another life, on another plane . . .

. . . she as the sand, him as the sea . . .

. . . him as moon, she as the stars . . .

. . . penguins . . .

About the Author

Bernice L. McFadden is the author of the national bestsellers *This Bitter Earth, The Warmest December* (short-listed for the Hurston/Wright Foundation Legacy Award), and *Sugar* (a Black Caucus of the American Library Association Fiction Honor Book). She lives in Brooklyn, New York, where she is at work on her fifth novel.